Take Me,
Take Me
with You

Take Me, Take Me with You

A Novel of Suspense

LAUREN KELLY

An Imprint of HarperCollins*Publishers*

Though some of the lore regarding antique clockwork mechanisms and mechanical dolls in this novel is fictitious, most of the historical information has been taken from Gaby Wood's *Edison's Eve: A Magical History of the Quest for Mechanical Life* (Knopf, 2002).

HarperCollins books may be purchased for educational, business, or sales promotional use. For information, please write: Special Markets Department, HarperCollins Publishers Inc., 10 East 53rd Street, New York, NY 10022.

FIRST EDITION

Designed by Joseph Rutt

Library of Congress Cataloging-in-Publication Data

Kelly, Lauren, 1938–
    Take me, take me with you : a novel of suspense / by Lauren Kelly.—1st ed.
        p. cm.
    ISBN 0-06-056551-9
        1. Women graduate students—Fiction. 2. Man-woman relationships—Fiction. 3. Suicidal behavior—Fiction. 4. Problem families—Fiction. 5. Revenge—Fiction. I. Title.
PS3565.A8T27 2004
813'.6—dc22

2003060439

04 05 06 07 08 BVG/RRD 10 9 8 7 6 5 4 3 2 1

To the legendary Otto

Take Me, Take Me with You

I

1

———

9 April 1971:
Lake Shaheen, New York

Are we going to see Daddy? Where is Daddy?
Momma? Where is Daddy?

This day at twilight when the sun appears soft as an egg yolk at the horizon a solitary car is observed descending route 39 into Lake Shaheen from the north. In this dense-wooded landscape in the foothills of the Chautauqua Mountains all horizons are fore-shortened. Vehicles appear suddenly around curves, rapidly descending into town, though this car, driven by a woman with a blurred face and long streaming hair, is being driven at about thirty-five miles an hour—a careful speed, a calculated-seeming speed as the car approaches the railroad crossing at the foot of the hill.

A quarter-mile to the east, the 5:48 P.M. Chautauqua & Erie freight is also approaching the crossing, much more rapidly.

Say you're the proprietor of Texas Hots Café. Say there's no customer in the café at just this moment, so you've been smoking a cigarette and staring out the front window of the café at nothing you haven't seen a thousand thousand times before. Not noticing still less giving a damn that the window is greasy, should be washed. Not noticing still less giving a damn that the asphalt in front of your café is beginning to crack, bad as the asphalt parking lot of the old train depot across the road; that weeds are growing in the cracks, like unwanted thoughts. Thinking that life is emptiness mostly—you managed not to get killed, blown up, or shot up too bad in the war—now your reward is, this emptiness at twilight of a day in early spring so cold and so cheerless it's indistinguishable from late winter, and even if a few more customers straggle into the café before you shut down for the night there's still this emptiness at the core, an emptiness you'd associate with Lake Shaheen, population 760, except you know it's elsewhere too, and anywhere: a stillness like the stillness between a faucet's slow drips. Yet so crowded sometimes, so much commotion inside your head there are moments when you can scarcely breathe, and you yearn for sleep to fill your head like soft warm concrete. All this while not really watching the car descending the hill toward the railroad crossing except to think with mild reproach *No headlights* but then it isn't dark yet, only just almost-dark, the sky overhead is vivid with waning sun and roiling clouds blowing down from Lake Ontario twenty miles to the north. You aren't aware that the car you're seeing is Duncan Quade's beat-up 1968 Chevy sedan he left behind when he moved away from Lake Shaheen sometime last summer, nor that the driver is Duncan Quade's wife, Hedy, who grew up around here, one of those Lake Shaheen High girls so pretty, so small-town sexy-glamorous that guys are all over them from the age of thirteen onward and they wind up married before graduating from high school, next thing they're mothers, and there's no next thing after that. Or anyway, no next thing they can see for themselves. And if their marriages go wrong, what then. But you aren't thinking yet of Hedy Quade or the likelihood that the small tense figure you half-see in the passenger's seat beside Hedy is probably the Quades' little boy, and behind Hedy in the backseat is a smaller child, probably the little girl. You don't know the kids' names: Duncan might've told you, but you don't remember the names of kids not your own.

And you aren't really watching the train yet. Except to note its lights are on.

This is the early-evening train, two passenger cars and the rest freight, coal and oil, the 5:48 P.M. through Lake Shaheen five days a week, that doesn't stop at Lake Shaheen but continues on to Port Oriskany fifty miles to the west. Truth is, you scarcely hear the trains any longer. You opened Texas Hots in 1946, back from the war (France and Italy, 1944–45) with a shot-up knee and a perforated eardrum and the trains passing the café and the shingleboard bungalow at the rear where you and your wife live are no more perceptible than pulse beats in your brain. People always asking how can you sleep through those damned trains and you just shrug, sure you sleep through the trains and so would anybody else in your position, anybody normal. If you'd been asked—as nobody of your acquaintance in Lake Shaheen or among customers likely to come into Texas Hots would ask—possibly you'd admit that you take comfort in the trains, their regularity east-west, west-east along the same tracks day following day. The locomotive whistle long and drawn out and melancholy, the clattering wheels. Vibrating of the earth at your feet. Especially you take comfort in the 5:48 P.M. because it signals the waning of the day and the coming of night which is your best time so you can sink back into sleep, head filling with sleep that no train whistle or clattering freight cars can penetrate.

Except today, a day you haven't yet noted has a date, is to be different. Tonight, you'll have a damned hard time getting to sleep.

Those mare's-tail clouds in the northern sky over Lake Ontario looking as if they'd been torn apart by angry fingers.

"Jesus. What?"

For there is getting to be something wrong. You're seeing it now. The steady speed of the car, the rapid approach of the train. Perpendicular lines, forces. Route 39, the raised railroad tracks. Instinctively you've been waiting for the car to slow. To brake to a stop at the crossing. You've begun to recognize the car, belongs to a local resident, Duncan Quade you're thinking though thinking too that you haven't seen the man in Texas Hots for a long time, nor anywhere in town; you haven't time to think *It isn't Quade, even drunk he knows better than to race a train.*

2

---

9 April 1993:
Institute for Semiotics,
Aesthetics, and
Cultural Research,
Princeton, New Jersey

Is this a mistake, is this a cruel trick. Don't ask.
I am not one to ask such questions.
I'm a scarred girl. I'm a marred girl. I'm damaged goods. I
take what I'm offered, usually. For I am not offered much.

The ticket to the concert was sent to me anonymously. There, in
a cream-colored envelope, fine paper stock, waiting for me in my
mailbox at the Institute. My name as I'd never seen it, in an elegant old-fashioned script, blue-black ink executed with a felt tip
pen—

L Quade

The rest of the address was typed, not handwritten.

I opened the envelope slowly. The secretary had told me there was something "very special" in my mailbox that morning, "looks like a wedding invitation." I'd murmured, confused, thinking that the woman was teasing me, "Oh, I doubt it. Not me."

My hand shook just a little, opening the envelope. There was no return address. The postmark was local. *L Quade* is not a name I would ordinarily be called in this place.

A single ticket fell out. Fell to the floor. Quickly I retrieved it, a pulse pounding in my throat.

It was for an upcoming performance in a local concert series, held on the university campus. This was a series of distinction which I sometimes attended but the seats I could afford were at the rear of the hall or in the balcony. This seat was C 22, center. A seat priced at forty-five dollars.

"A friend! Someone is my friend."

I smiled. I felt that I was being observed by the Institute secretary, perhaps by others. I wasn't yet suspicious. I wouldn't guess at the significance of the date until another time.

3

---

23 April 1993:
Princeton, New Jersey

He's hunting us. We have to escape him.
Hunting she'd always said. Your father is hunting us.
In the early 1970s before *stalking* had been invented and
promulgated by the media.

I went to the Friends of Chamber Music concert in Richardson
Auditorium on the Princeton University campus, there I was
shown to my plush-red seat C 22. Never before had I sat so close
to any concert stage. Never before in so privileged a position
where I would be able to watch a distinguished pianist's fingers at
close range.

I arrived twenty minutes early. Basking in the significance of
the occasion.

A friend, a friend! Who is my friend?

A young Japanese pianist would be playing that evening. Brilliant but controversial: his interpretations of classical piano
pieces, as of difficult contemporary music, were said to be
"radical"—"original."

Did I like it that other early arrivals were glancing at me, yes I did. That solitary girl midway in a row of yet-unoccupied orchestra seats.

A girl, you'd be led to think. Not a woman of twenty-eight.

An attractive, rather doll-like girl you'd be led to think. If you didn't come too close.

If the overhead lighting wasn't too bright.

I have to admit, I'd thought about exchanging the forty-five-dollar ticket for something cheaper. My stipend at the Institute—"stipend" was the term, not "salary"—kept me, like most graduate students, at just above the poverty line; and living in Princeton was not cheap. But I refused to give in. *No! You will not. This evening is a gift, you have an unknown friend.*

I wanted to believe this. I knew better, but still I wanted to believe.

For the occasion I wore a green velvet sheath that fitted my lanky body like a glove. A green velvet headband pushed my glossy black hair from my face. There was something very still and precise about me, like a doll in an upright, seated position; my face was a perfect oval. This oval had been shattered and mended in a filigree of near-invisible cracks, but as long as you remained at a distance—at least eighteen inches, depending upon the lighting—you weren't likely to know this fact.

What has happened to you?

Were you in a car crash?

When did it happen?

In fact it was rare that anyone asked, now that I was an adult. Living in a new part of the country where people tended to be polite, even formal. I'd endured public schools in Nebraska, Arizona, New Mexico and each morning now in New Jersey I woke to the relief of no longer being a child or a teenager; no longer being Hedy Quade's daughter.

Strange, the envelope had been addressed *L Quade*. In Princeton, at the Institute, I was known as *Lara Quade*; no one could have known that I'd once been *Lorraine Quade,* and that I'd changed my name as soon as I'd been old enough.

I might have changed my last name, too. But I had not.

He's hunting us. The three of us. His.

After more than twenty years, I doubted this was so. My father Duncan Quade had long vanished from my life. Mostly, he'd vanished from my thoughts. (Though I had a memento of his. Just one.) My mother had fled with us after the accident at the railway crossing and we'd never seen or heard from Duncan Quade since.

At least, I had not seen or heard from him.

We had our separate lives now. Hedy, Ryan, Lorraine/Lara.

Whoever had sent the ticket to *L Quade,* I assumed he was a music lover and maybe like me he favored the piano. Maybe, unlike me, he played a musical instrument. He'd noticed me at these concerts and possibly he knew me from the Institute where I was a research fellow and just possibly he took pity on me (I didn't want to think this, but it seemed logical) in my cheap balcony seats. He'd seen me from a distance of more than eighteen inches, and he'd liked what he saw. The glossy black hair, the perfectly poised head, an air of something withheld you might misinterpret as depth, integrity.

He was certain to be significantly older than I was and he was certain to have much more money than I had.

He was certain to be *he*.

The scars at my hairline were delicate as lace, you'd have to have a magnifying glass to see them clearly. Others, shaped like commas, on the lower part of my jaws and throat, you'd swear were slivers of glass still embedded in my skin.

Still other scars, brutal corkscrew twists of skin, of the sick color of curdled milk, were hidden inside my clothes, and these, on my back, my buttocks, my upper thighs, you weren't likely to see.

Jesus! What happened to you?

Car crash? Fire . . . ?

Still, I liked it that men's eyes drifted onto me sometimes in public places, and snagged like fishhooks. It wasn't my fault, I was blameless. I encouraged no one. I deceived no one. If I seemed to promise something I was not, the misinterpretation was not my own.

"Excuse us, may we—?"

I had to stand, to allow a couple to squeeze past me. The seats in Richardson Auditorium were old, handsomely refurbished but small, and the space between the rows was narrow, as if the old Gothic building had been designed for a smaller species of men and women.

The couple took seats C 21 and 20. Beside me, C 23 was still empty.

It was 7:50 P.M. The auditorium was filling steadily. Here and there were younger patrons, very likely music students, for there was a strong music department at the university and many performers and composers locally, but most of these younger patrons were seated at the rear of the hall and in the balcony, not in the front-row seats. Overall, the audience for serious music is an older audience: the average age in Richardson that evening must have been sixty. Patrons were subscribers to the series, well-to-do supporters of the arts. That tribe of Princeton patricians who were Caucasian, very wealthy, tastefully dressed and unfailingly courteous. I understood them to be good people: the kind of people Hedy Quade would identify, with a hurt little smile that hid her anger, as *money people*.

I understood that they were good people. The couple beside me, white-haired, elderly, fussing with their programs, their coats, the woman's handbag. *Not my benefactor. Not these.*

The Caucasian-patrician smell of women's discreetly lightened hair, expensive leather handbags, men's aftershave lotion and cologne. Seated among them I wondered if I might be mistaken for one of them: except I was conspicuously alone. If you belong to a tribe you are never alone.

Don't hate! Be grateful.

Scarred marred girl must always be grateful.

I think it must be because my mother had planned for me to die, with my brother Ryan and herself, at the age of six. You learn to measure living, the beat of your pulse, against that other: extinction. *Lorraine Quade 1965–1971* chiseled on the child-sized grave marker in a country cemetery in a wedge of upstate New York called Lake Shaheen.

If so I'd have been six years old forever. My brother Ryan would have been nine, forever. My mother, Hedy, thirty-one.

Thirty-one! So young.

He took my life from me. What's left now, isn't me.

It isn't me doing this now. It's what he has made me.

I was sitting in my plush-red seat and I was trying to concentrate on the program, reading about the young Japanese pianist who held the *Diplomino* from the Conservatorio di Musica in Bologna, Italy, his numerous awards and recitals and music festivals. This evening he would be playing sonatas by Samuel Barber, Bartók, Prokofiev. I was trying to read, trying to concentrate on the words, trying to drive away my mother's long-ago voice.

Remember I love you. You, and your brother.

"Do you come often to this series? My husband and I have been coming for twenty-six years . . ."

The white-haired couple beside me was trying to engage me in conversation. I had the idea that the woman, seated closer than her husband, had noted my damaged/mended face. The man was more likely to have mistaken me for a daughter of their tribe, oddly alone. In my green velvet sheath many times marked down and sold at $12.99 at the Second-Time-Around Shop just off Nassau Street, that might in fact have once belonged to a young woman of their acquaintance. In my green velvet headband that gave me the demure feminine look of a pre-Barbie ceramic doll. I tried to be polite but my replies were vague, faltering.

Never never show it. Nothing of what you feel.

For all I knew, maybe these were my benefactors. Wealthy eccentric music lovers who bought blocks of tickets to send out anonymously. If I was disappointed, I didn't intend to show it.

The seat to my right, C 23, was still vacant.

The house lights were dimming. The Japanese pianist appeared, brisk and somber, with a little bow glancing out into the audience as if to check, yes we were there, something alive and expectant was there, to mirror his dazzling performance.

Music is my other world to live in. Where I am not-known to myself. Where I have no memory. Where no voices from the past intrude, nor even my own. There, I become entranced. I am capable of feeling happiness at such times.

I have no talent for music, I think. No voice. Except I can recognize what music is or anyway what music is *not*: life.

Then, this happened.

A late arrival came, just after the first movement of the Samuel Barber sonata, to sit in C 23.

A clumsy figure. Graceless as a runaway truck down a steep incline. He sat so heavily, the entire row of seats shuddered. His knees were jammed tight against the back of the seat in front of him, jarring that row also, provoking people to glance back at him, annoyed. Shifting in his seat, that was too small for him, he poked me with his elbow. "Hey. *Sorry.*"

The dramatic mood of the opening movement of the Barber sonata had been shattered. As if a megaphone voice had overwhelmed a merely human voice. I felt my heart beat in disappointment, chagrin.

I'd wanted to believe that my anonymous benefactor would

be sitting in that seat. The measure of my disappointment made me realize this.

The intruder was a youngish ox of a man with unshaven, stubbled jaws and punk-style hair. No one associated with the Institute though (possibly) a graduate student at the university, an unorthodox composer or performer. He was panting, as if he'd been running. He gave off a smell like singed hair. His hard-looking head had been shaved like a skinhead's at the sides and back, but the rest of his hair was combed back long and lank and tar colored. His hands were big-knuckled, their backs covered in coarse dark hairs. As the pianist plunged into the second, forceful movement of the sonata, these hands gripped the man's knees as if to keep them from twitching; still, his left foot, close to mine, began keeping the beat, pushing just ahead of the beat. I felt such anger, a flame might have been lighted against my skin. *You don't belong here, why have you come here!*

I felt the danger of this individual as you feel the danger of standing too near the edge of a precipice.

Though you have no intention to throw yourself over. Yet, you feel the danger as a physical sensation.

I knew the tricks of mental discipline: I'd made myself into an almost purely mental person, since adolescence. I meant to concentrate on the pianist, and on the music; and I did. Avidly I leaned forward in my seat, to avoid contact with the stubble-jawed man. I stared at the illuminated keyboard, the pianist's agile fingers. The auditorium was filled with flawlessly executed musical notes like shattering glass. Here was power! Here was beauty. I would ignore the intruder beside me, my heart beat in disdain of him.

No one will cheat me of this.

I could feel the stubble-jawed man making an effort to relax. Hot-skinned, he seemed, and edgy. He must have felt clumsily out of place. He must have wondered why he was here. Now he sat with his arms folded tightly across his chest, holding himself in a kind of straitjacket. There was something wayward and careening about him that reminded me (uneasily, guiltily) of my brother Ryan whom I hadn't seen in years: poor clumsy short-tempered Ryan whose speech became slurred when he was excited, and whose left foot dragged when he walked, the result of minor brain damage.

This man was dressed like Ryan, too. Or what I recalled of Ryan. A well-worn leather jacket, unzipped. Khaki work trousers, hiking boots.

An anomoly, in this genteel Princeton setting.

Yet I managed to ignore him, mostly. The piano music was captivating. By degrees, I might have been alone in the auditorium beyond the brightly lit stage: there, the enormous Steinway concert grand piano dominated, and the figure of the very young-looking pianist with his remarkable flashing fingers. I was beginning to be placated, consoled. This was the place music brought me to. *If I can't achieve such beauty I need to know that others can.* The third movement of the Barber sonata was an adagio, precisely if rather coolly executed. The last movement was a bright leaping allegro, that seemed to me musically complex, intricate, and must be enormously difficult for any pianist to play. The percussive forward-motion of the conclusion had the drive of an accelerated heartbeat that left me breathless.

The sonata ended, abruptly. The pianist stood to accept his

applause. He bowed, now shyly smiling. How happy he was: you could see it now. That buoyant relief of having made his way through something treacherous.

Beside me, to my annoyance, the stubble-jawed man was clapping his ungainly hands, as if the music had meant something to him. Again his elbow collided with my arm.

"Hey, shit—I'm sorry."

He smiled at me. A twitchy belligerent smile, I thought it. As if he mocked me even as he feigned an apology.

The pianist exited the stage. In the interval before the Bartók sonata, the audience began to hum and buzz with voices.

Beside me, the stubble-jawed man made a show of peering at his program notes. " 'Samuel Barber. American composer.' Never heard of him, have you?"

Was he talking to me? I hardly glanced up from my program, nodding a vague cool reply.

"Takes getting used to, huh? That kind of music."

When I didn't reply he persisted. "Cerebal music, is it?"

"Cerebral."

The stubble-jawed man laughed at my correcting him. I couldn't tell if he was laughing at his mistake, or at my Princeton prissiness in correcting him.

"This guy, 'Okado'—'Okada'—he's pretty good, I guess? You heard him play before?"

I had to admit, I had not.

The stubble-jawed man shifted his knees, clumsy as clubs, against the back of the seat in front of him, and another time the woman sitting there glanced around at him, annoyed. He ignored her. He seemed to have taken a definite interest in me, out of boredom perhaps. I wondered that he hadn't left the concert after the first selection. "Weird, a Jap—a Japanese person—playing American music. *I* wouldn't."

I wondered if I was being prodded to ask: What music do you play, then?

I said nothing. My nostrils pinched against that smell of something singed, and, beneath, a yeastier odor of a man's body, dried perspiration, clothes not recently washed. I was reluctant to look this stranger directly in the face, knowing that's what he wanted. I was a challenge to his masculine vanity. I was possibly a puzzle to him: alone? And is she good-looking, or is there something weird about her face?

I wanted to protest *I'm not freaky like you. I belong here.*

The pianist returned, and began the Bartók sonata.

Bartók! Here was music that could frighten you, it was so percussive, obsessive. The pianist's hands hammered out chords rapid-fire. I thought it must hurt, such music. Perhaps it wasn't music but raw yearning sound. Beside me the stubble-jawed man, the man I wished to despise, stared at the stage and listened intently. His left foot kept the hectic beat. This was music you couldn't not listen to, it raced through you like neutrinos piercing solid objects. The Bartók piano sonata of 1926 was a powerful piece of music but it left me unmoved, only shaken; there was something chilling in its austere authority.

At intermission I thought *He will leave, he's had enough.*

I wanted this. And yet, I was anxious that the stubble-jawed man should depart, as abruptly as he'd appeared.

But he didn't leave. He stood by his seat, stretching his long legs and yawning. He was nerved-up, restless. This wasn't a rock concert—not quite!—but the Bartók had made his blood race. He glanced about the auditorium, squinting. I understood that he was keenly conscious of me.

On my other side the couple lingered in their elderly way in their seats. Chatting with friends in the row behind them as if the Bartók sonata had passed through their tastefully attired bodies leaving not the slightest trace.

I too stood, stretching my legs. I would have liked to walk up the aisle, I would have liked to pass among the chattering crowd in the foyer where the obsessive hammering of the Bartók piece had rapidly faded and was now not even an echo; there, I might see whether I knew anyone here this evening, and whether anyone knew me. A familiar face from the Institute, perhaps. *Lara Quade. Are you enjoying the concert I've arranged for you?*

Except my way was blocked.

I didn't want to stumble past the elderly couple, and I didn't want to push my way past the stubble-jawed man, who seemed to want to talk. I sensed an air of belligerence in his manner as if he felt, just maybe, someone was playing a trick on him.

" 'Bar-tók.' He's something, eh?"

I murmured, yes. I thought so.

"*You* play piano?"

I murmured, no. I did not.

"This 'Princeton.' You live here?"

I murmured a vague yes. It was true, I lived in Princeton for now.

As a research fellow at the Institute, I was a temporary presence. I had no permanent rank, title. We "fellows" laughingly called ourselves seasonal laborers. (In secret, each of us fantasized being kept on, or re-hired at a future time.) Some of us were serious about continuing our academic careers and some of us, like me, had possibly come to a dead end.

The stubble-jawed man stared at me, assessing. "What d'you do? Teach?"

A faint sneer to the word *teach*.

No one likes a teacher. I knew.

I shook my head ambiguously. Let this guy think what he wished.

Less and less likely now it seemed to me that my mysterious benefactor would identify himself. I had to suppose someone had bought a block of tickets and distributed them arbitrarily. This happened often in Princeton, though never before had I heard of tickets being given out anonymously; usually there was a patron, someone you were meant to thank.

The stubble-jawed man loomed over me. He was easily six feet three or four. Inside his worn mud-colored leather jacket he was wearing what looked like a black, much-laundered T-shirt with the logo of a rock band, unfamiliar to me. Heavy metal, I supposed it. I was reluctant to look at him too closely, knowing that he was watching me.

He was saying, as if this information might surprise me, "This is my first time here. 'Princeton.' I don't live too far away, up the Turnpike, but I never come here. It's not like other places in Jersey, huh?" There was a subterranean reproach to this remark; a craftiness that made me edgy. I so rarely spoke with strangers, I had no idea how to play the game of such casual-seeming yet shrewdly directed speech. For the stubble-jawed man was assessing me sexually, I knew. Yet so long as I rebuffed that knowing, and gave no sign of returning such an interest, I was free and clear of him. I believed this!

I hadn't wanted to be looking at him. Yet I saw a flash of a belt buckle: a silver Z.

He said, disdainfully, "*This* place, it's kind of old, I guess? Like, what?—a hundred years old? Two hundred?" He meant the auditorium, the elegantly refurbished Gothic building that was like a museum to enter.

I said I wasn't sure. Mid-nineteenth century, probably.

"Where I come from, old is just old. Here, old is a fucking big deal."

" 'Historic.' "

I was surprised to hear myself say this, impulsively. As I'd supplied the word *cerebral* earlier.

"Yeah, right—'historic.' Meaning M-O-N-E-Y. That's the big fucking deal." The stubble-jawed man laughed harshly, but with pleasure.

I lifted my eyes to his face, smiling. I felt weak suddenly, as if I might faint.

His eyes!—his eyes seemed familiar to me. Very dark and deep-set and rounded like a horse's eyes. There was a look of heat to them, as if thoughts beat hotly behind them; they were so dark as to appear black, and glistened strangely. I might almost have said hungrily. I had to wonder if he'd been noticing the scars at my hairline, beneath the pretty velvet headband; if he'd caught sight of the flurry of comma-scars at my jawline.

His own skin looked roughened, his nose was long and hawkish with dark cavernous nostrils. His mouth was fleshy, sullen-seeming, even when he smiled. For there was something ironic and withheld about his smile. *You believe this? Believe me? I'm a nice guy? You can trust me?* His eyebrows were coarse and wiry and nearly met over the bridge of his nose, giving him the primitive look of a mask carelessly shaped in clay.

I would think afterward: I didn't want to seem rude to him, that was it. He knew no one else there.

The surprise was, this man wasn't so young as you'd think at first glance, not twenty-five but in his early thirties. (My brother Ryan's age, if Ryan was still living.) His forehead was creased, one of his canine teeth had grown in at a rakish angle, scum-colored. His hot intense eyes fixed on my face, he was telling me how music meant a "helluva lot" to him since he'd been a young kid, music he'd hear on the radio, it was this secret place you could crawl into and hide and nobody could follow. He'd played in a band in northern Jersey for a while but gave it up, that wasn't what he wanted, other people in his face. Music was something he wanted for just himself. For his soul.

I wondered if I'd heard this correctly. I was feeling dazed, faint.

"Like sleeping really hard, y'know? That kind of dreaming, so hard it hurts, it's more real than real life, you don't remember what it is when you wake up but you sure remember— something."

The stubble-jawed man bearing the initial Z on his belt smiled at me as if goading me to say, Hey yes: I know exactly what you mean.

For some reason I said, instead, "But—why are you here, tonight?"

He smiled, shrugging. "Why? Somebody gave me a ticket."

The second half of the concert, a sonata and several short piano pieces by Prokofiev, passed in a rapid blur. I was conscious of the pianist's virtuoso playing and yet it seemed to me no more than a disjointed cascade of piano notes. *Somebody gave me a ticket.* The piano notes were confused with the pulse beating rapidly in my throat and the intimate presence of the man beside me. That smell of something singed, yeasty. I tried not to see out of the corner of my eye how the stubble-jawed man watched the pianist, frowning and grimacing. In the silence between musical phrases I heard his breathing that sounded unnaturally loud.

Somebody gave me a ticket.

The pianist exited the stage for the final time. My hands stung from clapping. I had the choice of following the elderly couple out of the row, or turning in the direction of the stubble-jawed man as he prepared to leave. Unconsciously it seemed, I turned to my right. I saw the man in the aisle, glancing back at me. His big rounded horse-eyes, with their unnatural glisten.

I intended to say nothing to him, simply to walk past him.

But I heard my voice lift in a shy, quick question: "You said—somebody gave you a ticket?"

Already he was fumbling in his jacket pocket. He brought out a cream-colored envelope, carelessly folded.

"Yeah. Weird! It came in this, in the mail."

I took the envelope from his fingers, he'd shoved it at me. It might have been the identical envelope in which my ticket had been sent to me. Except the handwritten name was different, of course—

Z Dewe

Beneath this was a typed address, a street in Metuchen, New Jersey. So that was where *Z Dewe* lived: an hour's drive away.

" 'Z.' For Zedrick."

Zedrick! I smiled at the name.

"Sometimes 'Zed.' "

I understood that I was meant to say *I'm Lara*. But I couldn't utter the words.

Yet I did something then that I would wonder at, afterward. At the time it seemed so natural I didn't hesitate.

I, too, had brought the cream-colored envelope to the concert, in my bag. In fact I'd been carrying it with me for the past two weeks, as if naively imagining I might see the handwriting replicated somewhere, and could identify it. Now I showed the envelope to Zedrick Dewe, as a child might show another child something of enormous interest to them both. "This was sent to me, with a ticket for tonight's concert."

Zedrick whistled thinly. I liked it that I could surprise this man, he had no idea who I was.

Zedrick took the envelope from me and examined it. I under-stood that he was memorizing my name, possibly; he'd know now that I could be found at the Institute for Semiotics, Aesthetics, and Cultural Research on Washington Road.

What a pretentious name! I wanted to laugh and assure Zedrick Dewe, yes I knew this was so.

Zedrick said, "Just the ticket inside? No note, huh?"

"Just the ticket."

He checked inside the envelope. To make sure I hadn't missed anything.

He said, "I figured, why not check it out? This thing tonight. It isn't my kind of music usually. But, see, nobody sends me any-thing, much. Kind of, I live alone. I keep to myself and for sure I don't know anybody in Princeton. But I can't figure it, what it means."

I said, "Maybe someone sent tickets out arbitrarily. For no reason. Taking names from a phone directory." Not that I be-lieved this, or wanted to believe it.

"Shit, why'd anybody do *that*? What sense is *that*?"

Zedrick Dewe was one who didn't like tricks played on him, you could see. He was roused to fury, at the prospect of being perceived as some sort of dupe, even of a beneficent act.

We were leaving the auditorium together. Outside, we de-scended the sandstone steps with numerous others who glanced at us curiously, especially at tall hulking Zedrick Dewe with his brutish hair, his stubbled jaws and odd clothing. I wondered if anyone from the Institute had seen us. I wondered if my appear-ance here, with so strange a companion, might be reported back to the Director. By this time I'd nearly forgotten my expectation, or my hope, that my anonymous benefactor would speak to me. I'd all but forgotten my benefactor.

In the presence of Zedrick Dewe, it was difficult to think of a purely notional being.

The night air was damply chilly. I slipped on my trench coat, I'd been carrying over my arm. I noted that Zedrick Dewe didn't help me with the coat as any Princeton man would have done, whether he knew me or not. I thought *In his world, you don't touch people casually*.

How like my parents' old, lost world. Upstate New York of a bygone era. Only dimly could I recall, I'd been so young a child then.

We were drifting in the direction of Nassau Street. But by an interior route. Like individuals who have no idea where they are headed so long as they remain together. Yet reluctant to leave each other. I might have mentioned to Zedrick Dewe that I lived about a half-mile away, I would be walking back home. Zedrick Dewe mentioned having parked close by. These were isolated remarks. These were remarks encoded with meaning. Swiftly my brain worked but could come to no conclusion. *I will have to get away from this man only just not yet.*

Crossing now a near-deserted quadrangle of the campus. This, the oldest part of the university. Here there was a flawlessly maintained green, tall trees, eighteenth-century buildings facing one another across a grassy space. Zedrick Dewe was saying, with the swagger of an intimidated man, that he'd "tried school, for a while" but quit because being told what to think, what to do, "pissed me off." I supposed that this was meant to impress me. I waited for him to ask me about the university, but he did not. Through his eyes I was forced to see familiar scenes subtly altered: the picturesque façade of Nassau Hall, illuminated at night by artfully placed spotlights, vivid and unreal as a stage set. Beyond, the yet more unreal Greek-temple façades of Clio and Whig Halls, startling white, like papier-mâché. High overhead, shreds of cloud were being blown across a quarter-moon that shone with unnatural brightness, like neon. I was tempted to tell Zedrick Dewe of the research I was doing for the Director of the Institute: amassing data on the earliest examples of "automata"— "humanoid" mechanisms.

But I could think of no way in to such remarks. No way that wouldn't threaten a man whom education has pissed off.

I thought *It's time: ease away from him.*

If he asked me to have a drink with him, I would say *Thank you, but—*

Yet we continued to walk together. As if we were headed for the same destination. Zedrick Dewe was less talkative now. His manner had become somber. So close beside me, he loomed taller than me by several inches. He must have weighed 190 pounds, approximately ninety pounds more than I weighed. I was beginning to shiver. Waves of exhilaration and dread rose in me, leaving me weak. I was hearing still the rapid-fire hammering of the Bartók sonata. My nerves were taut as piano strings.

If Zedrick Dewe had touched me suddenly, I would have recoiled from him.

We wandered into one of the few wooded areas on the main

campus. Along a drive bordered by tall trees. These were evergreens, there was a sharp smell of pine needles in the soft earth
underfoot. I led Zedrick Dewe across the grass and around to the
rear of the old, fastidiously restored Italianate house that had
been the residence of the university's president Woodrow Wilson
in an early decade of the twentieth century and was used now for
less elevated university purposes. Here was a garden, formal and
proper as a funeral, here were curving graveled walks and beds of
tulips of many colors that looked, by moonlight, like a single
color. "We should go in that direction," I said, pointing toward an
opening of evergreens around a corner of the Wilson house,
"back to Nassau Street. If—" I happened to touch Zedrick Dewe's
arm, the sleeve of his leather jacket. Instantly he took hold of my
wrist. His fingers were strong, closing about my wrist.

"Take me with you, O.K.?"

"Take you—where?"

"Wherever you're going."

The man's voice was urgent, pleading. But his fingers were
strong.

Overhead, the quarter-moon had shifted in the night sky. So
quickly, the moon moves in the sky. It had become a faint glowing shape nearly hidden by clouds. Wisps of cloud, shreds like
broken cobwebs or broken thoughts. If you had not known it
was a moon, you'd have had no idea what that curious glowing
object was meant to be.

4

October 1970: Lake Shaheen, New York

Where is Daddy, we asked.
Gone, we were told.
Abandoned us, we were told.
Hunting us, we were told.
Wanting to hurt us, we were told.
All that we knew of those confused days and nights was: our father was gone from our lives. And he would not return.

That night. The TV was on in the living room, TV voices mixed with sleep like strangers' voices in my head. I was wakened and so afraid, a man had hurt Momma, I knew. I thought I knew.

He's hunting us now, the three of us.

Cast his lot with swine. Worshippers of Satan.

Out of a sweat-prickly sleep I was awake hearing Momma moaning. Making a noise like something hurt then laughing. Except it's laughing you can't stop, laughing that turns into crying. Momma in the bathroom running water moaning and laughing to herself.

Beneath me in my lumpy bed was my doll Bessie, hurting my ribs. Bessie was my first doll. Bessie was a little girl like me except Bessie was a rubber doll with pink skin so soiled, and her head of silky black hair almost bald, and the pink of her tiny mouth mostly rubbed off, almost you couldn't see that Bessie was pretty any longer. *That sorry old doll!* Momma said disgusted. I had to hide Bessie from Momma, I was afraid Momma would throw Bessie into the trash.

Through the half-opened bathroom door I saw her: Momma bent over the sink trying clumsily to lift water in her cupped hands, to wash her face. Momma was shaking so, like a fit of shivering had seized her. There was blood on Momma's face, not bright-red blood but dried blood, and there was blood in Momma's hair. In the splotched mirror I saw Momma's eyes raw and swollen and scared, in the instant before Momma's eyes leapt to mine. There were bloodstains on the front of Momma's shirt with the tiny daisies that was like my shirt in the same daisy print, and one of the sleeves was torn at the shoulder.

I didn't want to think *Daddy has done this.*

I thought *A man has hurt Momma.*

Because since Daddy left, other men had come by the house. One of them on the front porch rapping his knuckles at the door calling out for Hedy to let him in, he knew she was home, her car was in the driveway, so let him in?

Sometimes Momma let them in, sometimes Momma did not.

Sometimes Momma sent us away to bed, sometimes Momma did not.

This night, I believed it could not be Daddy. I wanted to believe that.

Momma said that Daddy was gone from his rightful family and had cast his lot with evil, drug-takers and anti-Christs over in Good Hope forty miles away. On the far side of the lake it was. Abandoned us, Momma said. *Sleeps with swine. I hope to Christ you kids never see that sow. You'd be better off dead.*

It would seem to me, yes I'd seen them. I had!

Maybe it was a dream of Bessie's. Sometimes dreams passed from Bessie's head to mine. There were secrets between us. I could hear Bessie's voice though her mouth never moved. Her eyes on mine never moved. The dream was funny-ugly. Daddy and a big fat flush-skinned hog. Daddy sleeping with pigs in a trough now Daddy wasn't sleeping here in his and Mommy's jingly brass bed.

I started to giggle. I hid my mouth, giggling.

So silly! Why'd Daddy sleep in the pigs' trough with a big fat ugly old hog.

Ryan said, It ain't any old hog it's some lady.

Why'd Daddy want to be with some lady? Daddy is married to Momma.

Always Ryan knew more than I did. Ryan was eight years old, I was only five. Ryan was big for his age everybody said. Husky like Daddy and with Daddy's eyes and dark wavy hair. You want them to smile at you, you would do anything to make them like you.

That's why a girl is meant to be pretty: and to act pretty.

To make them like you. To make them not hurt you.

Momma's eyes on mine, in the mirror. Strange how you can see people in the mirror, at first they don't see you, and then they do. Not like seeing the back of Momma's head, where Momma can't see you watching her. But then her eyes lift, and there's a feeling like a match being struck.

"Go away! Bad girl! Bad Lorraine."

"Momma, are you hurt? Oh Momma—"

"Go away, don't look, this isn't for you to see, bad girl!"

"Momma—"

"Told you to stay in bed, what are you doing spying on me, you bad girl, you and your brother, where's your brother?—didn't I tell you to stay in bed till morning God damn you!"

Quick as one of those untamed cats that came by the house sometimes looking for food, Momma swiped at me with the back of her hand.

Not Momma's nails, just the back of her hand.

It was more the surprise of it, than the hurt. And the burning sensation in my cheek afterward like I'd been in the sun too long.

This night I would remember through my life but never comprehend. The way I'd seen Momma in the mirror before she saw me, and the blood on Momma's face she was trying to wash away with her hands, not wanting to use a washcloth or towel because she would soil it, and the blood in Momma's hair in a long vertical streak like a ribbon, and Momma's shirt with the little daisies. And Momma's eyes furious in the mirror in that instant she turned to swipe at me.

"Didn't I? God damn you, didn't I *tell you*?"

Memories like cards shuffled by a dealer whose face you can't see. Swift deft hands. Flashing cards. Dealt out onto a table.

One, two, three: cards dealt out, falling. No order to them.

What can you do but pick up the cards you've been dealt. Not wanting to think *Is this my life? And no order to it?*

Later I was in bed where Momma had carried me.

Momma muttering to herself, unsteady on her feet. "God damn! You would have to be a girl. I never wanted a girl. My mother had a girl." Momma laughed, stumbling.

Momma's breath had that smell. Sweet like wine, not sour like beer. The wine-smell, I liked. The other smell, that Daddy had on his breath sometimes, I didn't like. It made my nostrils pinch, and my eyes. And there was the smell of cigarettes on both their breaths, a cobwebby smell I didn't like.

I loved Momma and Daddy, though. I knew they loved me.

It was like Bessie. I had to discipline Bessie sometimes, for her own good I told Bessie. I had to hurt Bessie but I loved Bessie and Bessie knew. Why her hair was mostly gone, and her rubber skin scraped in places. But Bessie knew I loved her, and Bessie always loved me.

Like Momma didn't mean to hurt me when she slapped me, or shook me by the shoulders cursing me saying why'd I ever come into the world, when I cried Momma would stop right away like she'd been in a trance and was now waking, and she'd hug me and cry with me. Like she was ashamed. Like it was her own self she'd been hurting, and it scared her.

Saying now, trying to keep her voice level, "Lorraine, you must learn to obey your mother. We're not white trash. You and Ryan are not going to run wild. Now your father has abandoned us to cast his lot with swine everybody is watching, and waiting, to see what Hedy Quade is going to do, well, God as my witness Hedy Quade is not going to give in to despair, and Hedy Quade is not going to break down. You and Ryan, see, you're all I have and you're not going to turn into white trash. Especially you, Lorraine, a girl, you can't run wild, when you get older—" Momma was losing the thread of what she meant to say, now. Her wet hair was straggling in her face. She'd washed it in the sink and combed it through and cut away the dried blood with a scissors but she hadn't rinsed all the soap out, there were clots of white soap now. "—well, you don't want somebody to wring your pretty little neck, do you?"

I squealed Momma no! No no *no*. Because with no warning Momma was tickling me, closing her hands around my neck.

Just playing! Momma was just playing.

"Aren't you a squirmy little snake! Except snakes don't have any necks, do they? So how'd you wring a little snake's neck?"

Momma dropped me onto my bed stumbling and laughing. Squeezing her hands around my throat so that my eyes opened wide and there were splotches of black like sequins and I started to panic and kick and Momma relaxed her grip, it was O.K. Momma was only just playing, like Momma did sometimes. Her hands had that fresh-washed smell. Her fingers were slender and pretty and the nails were polished bronze-red except some of the nails were chopped, and broken, which wasn't like Momma, who hated that kind of slovenliness in a woman. So I knew that next day Momma would want to play beauty salon: I was allowed to file Momma's nails with an emery board, and I was allowed to polish Momma's nails if I took careful aim with the tiny brush, didn't act silly and didn't sneeze.

Then Momma might polish my nails, too. She did this for special days like Christmas, my birthday. When we visited Momma's family.

Saying in her boastful voice, Lorraine was her beautiful baby girl. See?

Saying, in her hurt angry warning voice, that was her newer voice since Daddy left us, Nobody is going to take her beautiful baby girl from her, not ever.

I hoped that Momma would sleep with me for the rest of the night, as Momma did sometimes now. Or, Momma let me crawl into the big jingly brass bed that was like a nest, with Momma's things mixed in with the covers, Momma's cigarettes, ashtray, chocolate-cracker boxes, taco chips. Momma and I would sleep off and on through the night, with the bedside lamp on. Momma had this thing she did with the lamp shade, she'd wind a scarf around it so the light would make the colors of the scarf glow. In the morning I would turn off the lamp while Momma was sleeping because it seemed wrong to me, to have a lamp on in the day.

In her sleep Momma twitched and moaned. Seemed like, she was arguing with someone. She'd wake suddenly not knowing where she was. She'd be afraid, that somebody was in the house, or in the darkened room with us. From her father, she was hoping to get a gun but he hadn't given it to her yet.

Giving Hedy a gun, no way.

Not Hedy! Not in the state she's in.

This, I'd overheard at my grandparents' house. My grandfather talking to my uncle Boyd. Not knowing I was close by.

Hedy has got to protect herself against him. She's got the kids to think of.

Who's gonna protect those kids against Hedy?

There was Ryan by the bed pulling at Momma's arm. Whimpering like he had one of his stomachaches or earaches. I knew— it was to take attention from me. I was sleepy now curled around Momma's hips where she was half-lying on my bed. (I tried to keep Bessie hidden so Momma wouldn't see and scold but Momma discovered Bessie right away. "Damn old Bessie! She's looking bad as I'm feeling.")

Ryan was asking in his whiny voice where Momma had been, he'd woken up and Momma wasn't anywhere in the house, and Momma said in her quick angry voice, "I never went anywhere. Never stepped foot out of this house. You two were in bed. You were both asleep."

Ryan said, "She was, but not me."

I knew that Momma's fresh-washed hands were twitching to grab hold of Ryan and I hoped this would happen. I was mad at Ryan for how he'd treated me that night. Tricking me into swallowing a mouthful of beer he'd gotten from one of Momma's half-emptied cans in the kitchen, put it in a glass saying it was apple cider. Right away it came into my mouth I knew it wasn't apple cider, it was nasty beer, I choked and spat it out and Ryan laughed and hooted at me.

Where Momma was at that time, I don't know. This long night beginning around ten o'clock when I should have been in bed, but wasn't. And now it was four o'clock in the morning! Those hours, I'd been sleeping sometimes, and awake others. But the times were confused with one another. Like warm syrup was leaking through my brain. Every time I was awake I was on the edge of sleep, but when I was asleep I didn't know where I was, what state I was in. Sleep has always scared me, it's a pit into which you can fall and fall and once you're falling you forget there was ever any other state than falling. Ryan was saying no he wasn't asleep, he hadn't been asleep but awake and he'd looked for Momma but Momma was gone and for a while they argued this, then Momma said finally she'd left the house, but she'd only been in the car, she hadn't gone anywhere.

Ryan said, "Momma, your car was gone, too."

"Damn you, it was not."

"It was! I saw it."

"You were asleep, you damn little brat. You were in bed, and you were asleep."

Ryan was panting. I hated how he'd nudged beside Momma on my bed, there was hardly room for Momma and me now Ryan was crowding in, too. "Momma, don't leave us, O.K.?"

Momma said, exasperated, "Ryan, I explained to you I didn't leave you tonight. Didn't I?"

"Or—take us with you?"

Momma sighed. Shifting her weight, and stroking Ryan's hot face.

"Honey, go back to bed. Enough of this."

"I'm not sleepy. I want to sleep with you."

"Well, you can't. You kick the covers. You make noises in your sleep, bad as your sister."

"I do not!"

Ryan's bed was on the other side of the room by the window. It was bigger than my bed. I hated Ryan crowding us when he had his own bed. But there was Momma sighing, with her arms around Ryan and me both. "Honey, don't worry. Your mother isn't going anywhere without you. If we wind up in the bottom of Lake Shaheen to escape that lying son of a bitch we will do that, the three of us, and we will be together, I promise. For eternity." Momma was speaking quickly now, her breath came faster. Heat lifted from her skin like the heat of sunburn. I knew that Momma was remembering something now, that she'd almost forgotten, but now she was remembering it, the way you become conscious of a noise you'd been hearing in the distance like an airplane or a train, and it jolts you into listening. Momma's voice was rapid and jittery and yet detached like a TV voice: "See, he tried to break in here tonight. He's a dangerous man. That woman he's with, she'll learn. Oh, she'll learn! Driven by lust. Swine. She'll regret stealing him from us. Maybe she has, already. Maybe it's too late for her. See, your father wants to come back now. He was here tonight. He wants to leave her, he said. You kids were in bed. You were asleep. You never knew. I went out, to stop him. He was parked on the road, his headlights off. He's done that other times. You never knew. This was late, this was past eleven. I knew I had to go outside to talk with him. I took a knife along— I was prepared! We were in his car. Daddy's car. That's where I was. I wasn't anywhere else. He's living across the lake in Good Hope, but he wants to come back to us. We drove around, he was crying. He said, 'I love you, Hedy, and the kids. I don't love anybody else.' I took a chance, I know. If he'd been drunk. Well, he'd been drinking but he wasn't drunk. Something in him was scared sober. Still, I had the knife. We drove to the lake, and back. Over the bridge, and back. I told him he could never come back into our lives, all he'd done to hurt us. I told him I would fight to the death for my children. He hit me, he hurt me, I never had a chance to use the knife, but I got away from him. I never used the knife. I'm not one to use a knife. He said, 'I hate her now, I'm scared as hell I'm going to hurt her.' I got out of the car, I got the door open and jumped out. I saved myself. I left the knife behind, in the car. I'd call the sheriff but those bastards are all buddies of his. He'd be one of them except the higher-up officers, the smart ones, took one look at Duncan Quade's record and shook their heads *No*. He wants to return here, he says. This is his home too, he says. He's working again, he says. I laughed in his face. I told him *No*. I told him he could grovel like a dog, it's his turn to beg. He said, 'But I don't love any other woman, Hedy. Only you. I made a mistake. Don't crucify me for a mistake.' He said, 'The first time I saw you, you were just a girl, I knew.' I just laughed at him. I hardened my heart against him. I never used the knife but it was like I sank that knife into his heart. And into her fat sow-heart. Never saw the sow's face, but I know of her. You bet I know of her. Duncan Quade cast his lot with swine and crawling back now on his hands and knees . . . See, I told him to go to hell. I told him, his soul is in hell. If he repudiates her, if he hurts her, that is on his head and not on mine. He hit me, tried to get his hands on me, I got the car door open and jumped out and I was laughing at him, I wasn't afraid because I knew that God would protect me." Momma was so worked up she didn't know what she was saying. Like her words were big and odd-sized in her mouth like stones. She was laughing now, but it was a sound like paper tearing.

This way, that night in October 1970, the three of us drifted into sleep.

Never would we see our father Duncan Quade again. Something happened that night, not even Ryan knew at the time. But it was that night. And ever afterward, all things were changed. But I'd taken Daddy's broken watch from the trash, before Daddy went away. He'd slammed his fist against a chair in the kitchen and sent it flying when Momma screamed at him and afterward his wristwatch was broken, the glass face was cracked and the tiny ticking had stopped. Momma scolded me, saying the cracked glass would cut my fingers, I couldn't have Daddy's watch, but later I found it in the trash and hid it away like I would hide Bessie from Momma. Ryan knew, but for once took pity on me. It was all I had left of Daddy.

5

---

24 April 1993:
Princeton, New Jersey

"This. I guess you could call it a talisman."

I was showing Zedrick Dewe the old, tarnished, broken watch. All the glass was gone now from the clock face, and the hands were twisted. Forever the watch was stopped at 11:17. The stretch band was gold-plated on the outside, aluminum or tin on the inside, and badly discolored. Yet how fascinating the watch, my father Duncan Quade's watch of almost a quarter-century ago. A brand I'd never heard of, *Lorus,* made in Japan.

My eyes stung with ridiculous tears. I was drunk: had to be drunk. Revealing to a stranger the pathos of my secret life.

Zedrick Dewe took the broken watch from me, weighed it in his hand. I had to think this was a gesture of politeness. We'd been recounting to each other something of our lives, in that detached way you tell of your life as if it's a tale meant to amuse, or to impress, possibly to seduce, but in the telling you're in danger of losing control of the narration like a car careening off a road at a sharp, unexpected corner and suddenly you've lost your

---

composure, your control, you stand exposed as if naked. Zedrick Dewe was shaking the watch gently, as if this would start it ticking. I saw a smudge of what looked like pale blue paint on his hand. He asked, "Your father's name was—is?—what?"

This was so unexpected a question, I answered without thinking.

"Duncan Quade."

A powerful name, I thought. A name I never spoke aloud, for no one would have known my father in my life now.

" 'Duncan Quade.' He's alive? Or—?"

Quickly I shook my head. This might mean yes, it might mean no. I'd revealed enough, I thought.

From what Zedrick Dewe had told me, his parents hadn't been married and he wasn't certain who his father was. There was a look in his face I understood. Raw and yearning. And resentful. *He wishes he knew his father's name* I thought. *He would give anything to know even the little that I know.*

But I'd revealed enough. My face was burning with a slapped sensation that was close to shame. Yet, as Zedrick Dewe stood staring at me, in my upstairs apartment at 23 Charter Street, at 2:20 A.M. of a rainy April morning, it was a half-pleasurable sensation, too.

I put the broken watch back in my bureau drawer. The uppermost drawer, where I kept my more fragile things.

"You live alone?"

That was Zedrick Dewe's first question, in my apartment.

Not that it was a question. Obviously, Zedrick knew. His deep-set cunning eyes glancing about the living room as I switched on the first of the lights. Still, I wanted to answer. To assert some measure of authority.

"Usually."

I'd brought a stranger back to my apartment. In Princeton, I had never brought any man back to my apartment. I had lived here for a year, but had not yet moved in fully. There were still books in cardboard boxes on the floors. There were improvised shelves made of bricks and boards, crammed with books. And a few dolls—my "doll collection"—mostly bought at flea markets and secondhand stores. Furnishings came with the apartment, and were spare and utilitarian though I'd draped some of them with shawls made of soft fabrics in beautiful muted sensuous colors. Around an ugly parchment lampshade I'd wound a strip of cobwebby magenta fabric, that gave to the light within a warm, intimate glow. I hoped that Zedrick Dewe would be impressed. I hoped that he would think that someone very appealing lived here. In my coolly speculative way allowing myself to think *This may be a mistake but it will be an interesting mistake.* I did not allow myself to think *This may be one of the great mistakes of my life.*

On the way here we'd stopped for a drink. After the drink we'd stopped at a wine and liquor store on Nassau, just as it was closing, and Zedrick bought a bottle of whiskey.

Seeing that it was difficult for us to detach ourselves from each other.

Seeing that Zedrick wasn't in any hurry to return to Metuchen, New Jersey. And I wasn't ready just then to be alone.

A sudden terror of being alone that night, when all other nights I was content to be alone. The feeling had begun with the violent percussive staccato chords of the Bartók sonata.

No no no no no the music protested.

In the tavern, amid raised voices and laughter, I'd told Zedrick Dewe my full name. He had seen Quade on the envelope, now I told him—"Lara Quade." As I uttered the words, they seemed to me fictitious.

I added, " 'Lorraine' was my name originally. 'Lorraine Anne.' I changed it—when I could."

Zedrick asked why I'd changed my name, I told him I didn't know.

Because that was her name for me. Because I could never hear the name without hearing her voice echoing inside it.

Strangely he said, " 'Lorraine' is a good name. Like you'd see on an old grave marker. In some country cemetery where it's all high grasses and thistles." Zedrick Dewe smiled, baring his discolored teeth. The canine tooth gleamed. I shivered, though I was smiling too. I could see that cemetery so clearly. "The last name, 'Quade'—that's a name you don't see much, huh?"

I said I didn't know. Maybe.

I supposed it was true: in our years of drifting across the country and back, Momma, Ryan, and me, we never encountered a single Quade, that I could recall.

Zedrick said, leaning toward me at the bar, as if confiding in me and not wanting anyone else to overhear, "I always liked my weird name. My hippie-mother named me. She'd named herself—'Jonquil.' Sometimes she'd call me 'Zed.' Like, a name for

Nothing. A name for Nought. I never needed to make up a name, when I was in a rock band."

We laughed together. I wasn't sure why. My single drink, a glass of white wine, had gone to my head. Zedrick, or Zed, was shaking my hand. I thought *My hand is being shaken by someone named Zed.* His fingers were warm and dry and strong. I felt that they could break my bones. I saw a sudden cloudedness in his eyes. A shadow like a fissure in his forehead. I felt weak, faint. Zedrick held my hand just a little too long, then released it.

Don't touch! Not just yet.

You'll know when.

In the kitchen alcove of my apartment I fetched glasses for Zedrick Dewe and me. I tried to keep my hands from visibly shaking. I wasn't skilled at drinking. After the single glass of wine my voice had become throaty, mildly slurred. There was a warm giddy glow to the edges of things that I knew to be, in fact, sharp. On the way to Charter Street I'd removed the green velvet headband and let my thick black crimped-curly hair shake free in the wind.

Zedrick wanted his whiskey straight. Me, I filled my glass to the top with ice cubes.

I was drawn to drinking even as I was fearful of drinking. I'd seen what drinking had done to my beautiful mother Hedy Quade who wasn't so beautiful by the age of forty. I'd seen what drinking had done to my father Duncan Quade. Already in junior high I'd had what was called a drinking problem. *Self-medicating* the school counsellor diagnosed it.

In time, Hedy would join AA. But not until both her children had fled her.

Zed opened the bottle of Irish whiskey and splashed liquid into our glasses. We touched glasses, we drank.

Liquid flame the Irish whiskey was, everywhere at once in my mouth and throat, rising into my nasal passages. I thought of my mean big-brother Ryan I'd trusted, years ago. *Go on. It's apple cider. It's real good.* I laughed.

What was funny, I don't know. My first male visitor upstairs at 23 Charter Street where I'd vowed I would bring no male visitor.

Yet: the man was Zed. *A name for Nothing. A name for Nought.*

I'd intended to play music for us. More Bartók, to intrigue and impress Zedrick Dewe who claimed to have played in a rock band in his early twenties. ("Guitar in the style of early Neil Young. But more ragged.") But now that we were alone together in my apartment I seemed to have changed my mind. The space was so small, Zedrick was restless prowling the room. He peered at book titles but made no comment. He peered at my modest doll collection. Why'd an adult woman choose to display such things? His expression was quizzical, possibly pitying. *A doll to an adult woman is the baby she doesn't have.* I told Zedrick, though he hadn't asked, that the dolls were whimsical purchases, not especially valuable, old but not "old."

"This one, it's a wind-up?"

Zedrick had discovered Tina who was eight inches tall, a beautiful little girl with wavy blond hair, sparkly blue eyes, rosebud lips and a flawless rubber skin, unfortunately missing her left arm. Tina wore a white, slightly soiled satin gown with lace trim that looked disconcertingly like a wedding gown. I'd bought Tina at a church rummage sale here in Princeton, for $3.

I wanted to ask Zedrick not to wind up Tina, please put Tina back on her perch and let's forget Tina, but there was Zedrick cranking the wind-up mechanism and after an awkward hoarse start Tina made a cooing sound that might have been "Ma-Ma" through her frozen rosebud lips. Tina fluttered her thick dark eyelashes though her bright eyes remained glassy and unfocused, and Tina moved her remaining arm in a jerky upward-downward motion.

"My mother Jonquil, I was telling you?—she made Raggedy Ann dolls. Mostly she grew pot, though." Zedrick laughed, replacing Tina on her shelf. "Jonquil was quite the hippie."

I wondered at the way Zedrick said *was*. With such finality.

"Jonquil isn't living now, if you're wondering."

"Oh. I'm sorry."

Zedrick shrugged. "She brought it on herself, people said. I kind of blamed her, myself. Dying young."

I bit my lower lip. I couldn't say again *I'm sorry*!

"I don't think of Jonquil much anymore. There was a time, I thought of Jonquil every minute. I was nine when she died, the last I saw her was the morning of the day before she died, she was sending me off with some friend of hers and her kids. I didn't want to go, but Jonquil made me." Zedrick paused, drinking Irish whiskey. Almost, I could see the amber flame behind his moist eyes. "Jonquil was a big, beautiful woman. White-blond hair in plaits to her hips. Like a girl in a picture book. She went barefoot everywhere in the summer, her feet splayed out, she couldn't get the dirt out from under her toenails. She was a pothead, her and her hippie friends. They grew marijuana and sold it and sometimes they got into trouble and that wasn't so good."

"Where was this, Zedrick?"

Zedrick shrugged. He gestured with his arm as if it didn't matter where, somewhere north of here.

"And your father? Is he—alive?"

Another time Zedrick shrugged. His expression was unreadable.

"My father, if it's the one people thought it was, and Jonquil told me it was, he tripped out when I was born. He went away, and later he came back to live with us, but it was almost too late. It was too late." Zedrick paused, drinking whiskey. He seemed to be considering, if he should tell me these things; if he, too, might be exposing too much of himself.

"When was this, Zedrick?"

"Back in the early 1970s. People didn't get married then, or anyway some of them didn't. They lived in beat-up old farmhouses and raised their kids in 'communes.' They were well intentioned I guess, that's the best you could say about them. And not all of them were well intentioned. They left cities and went to live in places where they didn't know anyone, and the locals hated them. The Vietnam War hadn't ended yet. Lots of Americans hated one another on principle as well as the fact they hated one another's guts. But Jonquil was a 'flower child' as she called herself. *She* wasn't going to be touched by anyone's hatred."

Zedrick spoke with adolescent sarcasm. I could see how he

resented his mother still, for leaving him. How he loved her, and was hoping to forget her.

I would have liked to ask Zedrick more but this wasn't the time. I saw his face shutting up. I thought *You can open up a man just so far. Farther, he's dangerous.*

We talked about easier things. I asked Zedrick what kind of work he did, and Zedrick said he worked in a photo lab, it was temporary until he could get something better. Living in Metuchen, New Jersey, was temporary, too.

Zedrick asked me what my work was, and I told him: I was a research fellow for the Director of the Institute with the pretentious name, and I spent between eight and ten hours a day in the library, or at a computer terminal. Zedrick asked what kind of research and I hesitated, reluctant to say. "Basically, it's research into early automata, clockwork mechanisms like mannequins, dolls, what we now call 'robots.' "

Zedrick frowned. He'd heard of robots, sure.

Because I was reluctant to talk of my work, my work that seemed to me both fascinating and perverse, and, in my own life, pointless, labor exclusively aimed for the use of the Director in his newest project, I behaved as if I had nothing to hide; as if I took delight in my work; I showed Zedrick photographs in several books including reproductions of the infamous automata of Jacques de Vaucanson (the Flute Player, the Pipe Player, the Soprano). "This was eighteenth-century France. It was an intensely Catholic society. When Vaucanson's androids performed, they seemed to spectators 'real.' And Vaucanson used real skin on them, probably human skin."

Zedrick stared at the photographs in the frayed old book titled *Les Automates: monstres et prodiges,* that had been published in Paris in 1879. He sucked in his lips. I could see that something offended him. " 'Automata'—that's what these are? They look pretty real."

"Except the eyes. People could tell, seeing the glassy eyes, that they weren't real."

Zedrick laughed. "Lots of people I know, they've got glassy eyes."

Zedrick leafed through the book, pausing at other plates. I wondered what he was thinking of my research: what was the point of it, delving into the past; and why was I involved in it. I said, "The Uncanny, Freud called it. The sensation we have when we see a mannequin or a waxwork figure that's so life-like we think, on an instinctive level, that it must be alive like us."

Afterward I would wonder why: why *Freud,* why *instinctive level,* why displaying my knowledge like this. What bullshit it must sound like to a man like Zedrick Dewe who had not (I seemed to know) attended college, still less had a graduate degree as I had.

Zedrick made a derisory sound, and let the book fall shut. A small explosion of dust lifted from it; the last time *Les Automates* had been checked out of Princeton's Firestone Library had been 1969.

Zedrick's eyes lifted to mine. I shrank a little at their dark glistening intensity, yes it was a glassy intensity, on the edge of mockery, and it made me shiver.

Here is the Uncanny.

Zedrick said, drinking, "Like looking at somebody who's freaky somehow. Like, disfigured. Scars, or an arm or a leg amputated. Some people get off on it, you know?"

It wasn't a question. I felt my face heat at the reference to scars.

He knows. He has seen. He finds me repulsive.

I laughed uneasily. I felt as if this man, taking up so much space in my cramped living room, seated facing me on a chair, was tickling me with rough careless fingers as, long ago, my Daddy had done.

"Dolls. They're weird, too. Baby-sized. *You* look like a doll, Lorraine."

"My name is Lara. Not Lorraine."

"O.K., Lara. Lara-doll. Anybody ever tell you, you have a face like a doll?"

"I look weird, you're saying? That isn't very flattering."

I tried to speak matter-of-factly. With an air of confidence I didn't truly feel. As I did frequently at the Institute, in the presence of my distinguished elders and my younger rivals.

Zedrick amended, "Weird-pretty, like a doll. There's no ugly dolls, are there?" He regarded me in silence for a long moment. Aggressively, with no effort to disguise his sexual interest. At the same time I believed he was being playful, even affectionate.

Always, you want to believe this. Sexual. Playful. Affectionate.

"Maybe it's because I collect dolls." I laughed, I was feeling giddy. I tried to sip whiskey but my eyes blinked rapidly as if I'd leaned too close to an open flame. "Maybe it's because I had a doll I loved when I was a little girl, and she died in my place in a car crash."

Zedrick was sprawled in a chair facing me. His grungy jacket he'd removed and tossed over the back of the chair. His ropey biceps stretched the tight short sleeves of his T-shirt and the silver *Z* at his belt flashed with an aggressive light. He'd become alerted as I had known he would. "Car crash?"

I considered how to tell this. The truth was, Bessie had disappeared several days before the crash. I'd wakened one morning and Bessie was gone from my bed and gone from every hiding place I knew and my crying would not bring her back and my child-despair would not bring her back and my whimpering to Momma would not bring her back, not ever. But it was more dramatic to claim that Bessie had died in the crash in my place.

Zedrick persisted, "Car crash? When?"

I made a vague troubled gesture. Meaning, a long time ago.

I drank. The amber whiskey flooded my mouth and delicious it seemed to me, and dangerous. Beneath me the floor began to tilt. The scuffed maple floorboards beneath my braided rug. If it shifted much more, I was in danger of toppling from the edge of the wicker sofa where I was sitting not four feet from Zedrick Dewe.

"It was an accident. No one died."

I hadn't meant to utter this as irony. *It was an accident, no one died.*

It was an accident, that no one died.

Zedrick said, "Tell me."

Tell him! How badly I wanted to tell him.

Wanting to stroke the man's stubbled jaws. Wanting to stroke his lank tar-colored hair. Wanting to feel his arms around me. Even the risk of it, the danger.

"I was six. I was in the backseat of the car. My mother was driving. My brother Ryan"—for I had to include Ryan, I could not omit Ryan if I was in the backseat of Momma's doomed car, who but my brother would be in the passenger's seat, shrewdly I knew I must be as accurate as possible if I wanted to convince Zedrick Dewe of the veracity of my words even when I departed from veracity—"was nine, he was in the front seat and so he was more seriously hurt than I was because the car sideswiped a train on the passenger's side—"

"Sideswiped a train? You mean, a moving train?"

"A fast-moving train."

My eyelids fluttered like a doll's. My eyelids closed. It was a way I had: not entirely conscious: a way of controlling the tilting sensation. At the same time, my face was a mask of affable composure, like a subject under hypnosis. I heard the wind outside the car windows, and I heard the deafening locomotive whistle, and I saw the headlight, and I saw the train rushing perpendicular to the highway ahead of us; I saw the blurred side of our mother's face, waxy-pale and without expression, adamant. She had made her decision. Hours before, she had made her decision. A call had come for her. A single call. I'd heard her cry out as if she'd been struck to the heart, I saw the telephone receiver slip from her hand and fall with a loud noise to the kitchen floor, then dangle comically at the end of its rubber cord. I heard, and I saw. I did not question. Now in the car, descending the hill into

Lake Shaheen from the north, I heard screaming. The piteous pleading screams of children. But the woman with the beautiful waxy-pale face and wind-whipped wheat-colored hair in the driver's seat was silent, and unhearing.

"My mother was driving down a long hill. And she lost control of her car, it was an old car and the brakes were bad and the road was wet from rain or—ice—'black ice' it's called—when the surface of a road first freezes, and you can't see it. This was in Lake Shaheen, New York. A small town you've never heard of in the Chautauqua Mountains. The train was coming along the tracks, it was almost at the crossing before my mother saw it, there was no gate at the crossing, no warning lights, this was a country crossing, and my mother slammed on her brakes and the brakes didn't hold and she turned the steering wheel to the left and the car skidded sideways and struck the train in the direction in which the train was traveling, and the car was dragged for hundreds of feet twisted up under the wheels before the brakeman could stop the train." I paused, I could hear my panting breath. I felt dazed as a tightrope walker who has crossed her tight-stretched rope without falling to her death and now awaits some sort of applause. It was true, I'd told distilled versions of the crash several times, each time to men, but this was the first time I'd introduced *black ice* which seemed to me an appropriate detail, one I would want to use again. It was true, too, that I remembered virtually nothing of the accident beyond the impact of the skidding car against the train; if I knew that the mangled wreck of the car had been dragged for hundreds of feet, it was because I'd been told. I would not regain consciousness for a day and a half, and would wake in the intensive care unit of Port Oriskany General Hospital fifty miles away.

Possibly my memory never returned, entirely. Possibly it's futile to make the effort of remembering.

"Anyway," I said, trying to smile, "no one was killed."

Zedrick whistled thinly through his teeth. I saw that I had impressed him.

"An accident, you say? Weird."

"The brakes on the car were old. The pavement was icy . . ."

My voice trailed off faintly. I fumbled to drink Irish whiskey as Zedrick Dewe regarded me with an expression that might have been sympathetic, or might have been skeptical.

Falteringly I said, "It was a long time ago. I rarely think of it now."

Twenty-two years. Enough!

Yet Zedrick persisted. "Your brother was hurt pretty bad, you said? Is he O.K. now?"

"Yes."

I couldn't admit that I had no idea how my brother Ryan was. I hadn't seen him in twelve years since he'd entered a drug rehab program in Phoenix, Arizona. Guiltily I told myself *If Ryan needs me I would know it.*

"And—your mother?"

I was losing the thread of the conversation, staring at Zedrick Dewe's glistening eyes.

"What about my mother?"

"She's alive? You're in contact?"

"Yes."

Yes. But no.

I wasn't sure. I hadn't spoken with Hedy Quade in more years than I cared to recall.

This man wants a way in I thought of Zedrick Dewe. *A way in to my life.*

The thought excited me, and filled me with unease.

Naively I told myself *Zedrick Dewe will love me. I won't let myself love him.*

His forehead was prematurely lined, in horizontal creases like something made with a knife blade. He had a habit of grimacing, rubbing his knuckles against his face. As if thinking pained him. As if he didn't like the things he was obliged to think.

"People do weird things to their children. The weirdest part of it is, if you ask them why, they'll tell you they don't know what the hell you're talking about." He paused, drinking. I wanted to protest *But it was an accident! I told you.*

We fell silent. The rapport between us shimmered and quaked like air agitated by heat waves. Again I felt a powerful urge to touch Zedrick Dewe, and to be touched by him.

I said, as if we'd been arguing, "There isn't always a motive for an act. There can be accidents."

Zedrick nodded. Sure.

"Or there can be so many motives, it's like saying there is no motive."

Zedrick considered this, and drank. I wanted to smooth the creases in his forehead with my fingertips.

"Sometimes I think . . . But I guess I shouldn't say it."

"Say what?"

"That life itself has no motive. We seek a motive, but it's futile. We seek meaning, and there's nothing. The shallows of life are as significant as its depths."

Unconsciously I'd been fingering the comma-scars on the underside of my jaw, that flared up like a rash when I was feeling strain, or uncomfortably warm. Almost, I could think that the glass slivers were still inside.

In the dark, a lover wouldn't see the worst of my scars. He would feel them, though.

Zedrick said, "Hell, think of it this way, honey: you didn't die in the crash. You were lucky."

I smiled. I wanted to believe this.

"You're right, Zedrick—I'm 'lucky.' "

"And where was your father? At the time of the crash."

"They were divorced by then. I think. I don't know where he was." I paused, rubbing at my jaw. I would like to have dropped the subject.

"Did he come to see you in the hospital? Any of you?"

"He—might have. I don't remember."

But of course Duncan Quade hadn't come to see his family in the hospital. Not Momma, not Ryan, not me. I seemed to know (from remarks made in my presence by adults speaking in a kind of code) that Duncan Quade no longer lived in the Shaheen/Good Hope area, but in another part of the state.

As soon as we were discharged from the hospital, Momma packed the three of us into a camper she'd bought from a relative and we left upstate New York forever. Months and eventually years of traveling in a southwesterly direction *on the road* as

Momma called it. Never another permanent home. Never any contact (that Ryan and I knew of) with *back there* as Momma spoke bitterly of her past.

I told Zedrick Dewe nothing of this. I wondered if, like my mother Hedy Quade, I was deeply ashamed and my shame had turned to rage without my knowing.

There stood Zedrick Dewe hovering over me. He fumbled for my hands that were brittle as ice. "Hey: don't cry. The crucial thing is they tried, honey, but they couldn't kill you."

Honey. My heart beat rapidly and shallowly as a doll's clock-heart.

I wanted Zedrick Dewe to drop to his knees in front of me, or to squeeze beside me on the sofa, and close his arms around me. I sensed how close Zedrick Dewe was to doing this. Yet I sat stiff and unyielding as a mannequin, trembling, frightened. My smile felt stitched into my face.

Zedrick said, still crouched over me, "I'm 'lucky,' too. If my mother hadn't sent me away that day, I'd have been home when she was killed. I'd have been killed, too. With the same knife."

Before I could react, Zedrick backed off. Maybe he was thinking he'd exposed too much of himself, too.

Saying he needed to use my bathroom. Not asking where it was, the apartment was so small.

Afterward I would marvel at what I did next. When Zedrick Dewe was in the bathroom and I could hear the hot hissing stream of his urine through the shut door, I rose unsteadily but eagerly to my feet, went to the chair he'd been sitting in and took his leather jacket and slipped it on. How heavy it was, and how bulky! A dull old-leather smell, and a hide the color of mud, finely cracked and creased like glazed pottery. The wrists of Zedrick Dewe's jacket fell to my fingertips. The waist drooped below my hips. I shut my eyes inhaling its smell.

A man's leather jacket has numerous pockets. Some of them are visible, others hidden. Most can be shut up tight with zippers. As the sound in the other room of my guest's streaming urine reached its noisy peak and began to wane, quickly I unzipped pockets, quickly I thrust my hands inside. In the right side pocket was a pair of leather gloves. Wadded-up tissues in other pockets. And the folded cream-colored envelope with the elegantly handwritten Z Dewe on its front. A box of matches. A stub of a pencil. Loose change.

I would have liked to take the envelope. Instead I took the little box of matches, and hid it away in a desk drawer.

I replaced the jacket over the back of the chair where it had been tossed. Like a shed skin. Not new, not very attractive yet oddly sensuous, to my eyes beautiful.

He's going to hurt me. He can't help it.

When Zedrick Dewe returned to the living room, the mood between us seemed to have altered.

Like the highly charged air before an electrical storm. Where there'd been tenderness in Zedrick's manner, now there was tension.

Where he'd been patient, asking me about myself as if nothing could interest him more, now he was impatient. Asking if I wanted more whiskey, and I said, laughing, "I'd better not, thanks," and pouring whiskey into his glass, and drinking, standing before me like a preening male, suddenly aggressive. The very stubble on his jaws seemed to have darkened. His mouth looked hungry as a pike's. As if, alone in the bathroom, he'd caught a glimpse of his damp flushed face and hadn't liked what he saw. *Fuck her, or give it up. This is taking too much time.*

What happened next is confused in my memory. As in a car crash you remember mostly pieces, fragments. Memory itself has been broken.

I remember Zedrick coming to me where I was sitting at the end of the sofa, and he may have made a remark about "more dolls" in the bedroom, he'd stepped through that room on his way to the bathroom and he'd seen three or four dolls on the windowsill, or maybe he joked about my resembling a doll, or being a doll—"Lara-doll." His tone was teasing. I didn't want to think it was sneering.

Telling myself he wouldn't be speaking to me like this if I hadn't invited it. Through the evening, back in Richardson Auditorium, crowded in the seat beside him, I'd invited it.

Very deliberately he framed my face in his hands. I began to tremble as soon as he touched me. For these were big hands, a man's hands. Capable of exacting harm. If he wanted to turn my head swiftly and savagely he could have broken my neck and, yes there was this realization between us, as sudden and startling to the man as to me, not that Zedrick Dewe was going to break my neck but there was this knowledge unspoken between us, a flame passing between us. I'd stumbled to my feet to lessen the tension on my neck where Zedrick was tugging at me, and Zedrick kissed my mouth, and kissed me harder, forcing my mouth open.

We staggered apart, panting. Staring at each other like drowning swimmers caught in the same roiling wave.

"I think—I—"

But I could not speak. I was excited, and I was apprehensive. I knew that my eyes were dilated and that my skin was hot, flushed. I felt the injustice of it, to be teased as *Lara-doll* because I resembled no doll now.

Zedrick grabbed me, and squeezed my breasts through the green velvet dress; he tugged at the straps, and his hand were everywhere on me, impatient and rough. He gripped my back, my buttocks. He pressed himself against me. His aroused heated body. Hungry pike-mouth. We'd passed beyond seeing each other. That dangerous point, beyond which you cease to see the other. I smelled his breath, his body. I tasted his whiskey-saliva. His probing tongue filled my mouth. His fingers would leave their imprint on my flesh, bruises to darken, turn a faint rancid orangish hue, lingering for days.

I thought of Momma: the rough tickling games. Making me laugh, making me squirm, kick, squeal. That moment when being tickled turns into being tormented. That moment when childish ecstasy turns into panic. How then Momma would laugh in reproach, reassuring me that I was safe, I was loved. *You know you're Momma's beautiful baby girl—don't you?*

Zedrick was pulling me in the direction of my bedroom. I didn't panic but I did resist: "No. Wait."

"What? You want this, baby. Don't tell me you don't."

The man was drunk, he'd become a drunk and a bully and I pushed away from him. My face burned as if he'd slapped me. My mouth, and my breasts, throbbed with pain.

A mistake, a mistake. You are to blame, this is a mistake.

Zedrick Dewe's crude words repelled me. I saw that he was hurt, and he was angry. And he was drunk.

"Why'd you ask me back here? Cocktease."

It was juvenile. It was happening so swiftly, I could not quite believe it.

Zedrick fumbled to snatch up his leather jacket from the back of the chair where I'd positioned it so carefully. He turned to leave. His face was sullen, hateful. I felt a stab of guilt and touched his arm and stammered, "Zedrick, wait—" and something in the man exploded, he cursed me in a low furious voice and he grabbed my shoulders and shook me hard, hard, hard and I was too stunned to resist, too dazed to cry for help.

He will hurt me now, that's why he has come here.

Not then but later I would think *That's why I brought him here.*

I was strong for a woman of my weight and height but not so strong as my assailant. I was quick and frantic to defend myself as a feral cat trying to claw at Zedrick Dewe, kick at him. But he was too strong. He shoved me aside, I backed away, shielding my head and shoulders. "Cunt," he was saying, almost in fury his voice became tender again, "think you're hot shit, huh?—too good for me." The roaring in my ears was deafening, I could barely hear. I seemed to be viewing the scene, a clumsily enacted TV scene, from a distance. With an extravagant sweep of his arm this man I'd invited back to my apartment where never before had I invited any man knocked books from my desk, knocked my computer keyboard to the floor, overturned a desk lamp. Overturned the part-filled whiskey bottle. Struck at the dolls on their elevated shelf, sending poor astonished Tina flying across the room. On his way to the door he kicked aside a chair.

"Fuck yourself, Lorraine."

On the stairs his footsteps were heavy. Within seconds he was gone.

A scarred girl. A marred girl. Take what you are offered, you are not offered much.

I staggered to the door to lock it after Zedrick Dewe. I had not realized how terrified I was. For long minutes then lying amid broken things and the sickly sweet smell of spilled whiskey. My head felt as if it had been kicked. My eyes leaked tears of shock, shame. The green velvet dress of which I'd been so vain was torn, stained with a man's oily sweat where he'd rubbed his face against it. On my breasts I would discover reddened marks and discolorations, on my thighs, buttocks, back I would discover ugly bruises. Beneath my bed was an object that turned out to be Tina broken on the floor. When finally I had strength enough to make my way into the bathroom to wash my face I saw in the mirror that my upper lip was swollen and bleeding, a bruise had formed above my left eye.

He didn't hurt you as he might have. He did not rape you, he did not strangle you. You are alive.

6

August 1970:
Lake Shaheen, New York

"Daddy! Dad-dy!"

Running! In the driveway, and on the road after Daddy's departing car. In the wake of the accelerating motor of Daddy's departing car. In the exhaust of Daddy's departing car that made us cough, choke. Shrinking red taillights of Daddy's departing car.

My brother ran faster than I could run, my brother was eight years old and I was only five. Daring to duck past Momma who stood in the doorway and grabbed at our arms, our hair. Momma screaming our Daddy would kill us if he saw us, if he got his hands on us, didn't we know our Daddy was drunk, didn't we know our Daddy was dangerous—"Shame your father in the eyes of the world, he'll kill you!"

It was a muggy summer night. Gnats and mosquitoes swarmed hungrily. Gnats in our eyelashes, on our lips and sticky skin. When we had no more breath to run, when we stood panting and sobbing in the road, mosquitoes hummed in our ears and settled on our exposed skin, bit us and sucked our racing blood.

Momma's voice was faint in the distance. Momma's voice like the cry of a loon on Lake Shaheen.

That was the night it began.

The night what began?

All of it. What he did, what she did. What was done to us.

When we ran after Daddy, you mean. That night Daddy moved out and left us.

It was a later time. Almost a decade later. I'd gone to see my brother, Ryan, in the infirmary of the Men's House of Detention, Phoenix, Arizona. My brother Ryan was a heroin junkie. My brother Ryan who'd survived the car crash with injuries to that part of the brain known as the cerebellum was nineteen years old and looked forty. Minutes after I'd been escorted into the infirmary and to his bedside by a guard we began to quarrel quietly, stubbornly.

No. I ran after Daddy, by myself.

Ryan, no. I was with you. I ran after Daddy, too.

Like hell you did, Lorraine.

I did! I remember.

Momma grabbed you by the hair, and kept you back. You were just a little girl.

But I remember.

No. I was alone. I ran after his car, and if he saw me he never slowed. If he saw me he never gave any sign. I was calling to him

Daddy stop! Daddy take me with you! *but he never heard, he accelerated that car from zero to sixty miles per hour in fewer seconds than it takes me to tell it.*

Ryan, no: I was with you. I was running after Daddy, too.

You weren't, Lorraine. But if you want to remember it that way, maybe you should.

7

April–May 1993:
Princeton, New Jersey

He won't be back. He despises you.
This was my consolation.

Those days and weeks after. Alone in my apartment with the door barricaded or making my way cautiously through the labyrinthine stacks of the university library or in the presence of others, my colleagues at the Institute and the director himself— "Miss Quade? I'm afraid this addendum has to be redone, I have more material to include"—I had only to listen to hear Zedrick Dewe's sneering yet somehow caressing voice. *Cunt. Hot shit. Lorraine. Fuck yourself.*

That night. Lying amid the broken things for long dazed minutes then dragging myself into the bathroom and in the bathtub I lay in scalding soapy water to cleanse my body numbed as the body of an accident victim. I may have smiled, in a rapturous daze.

"I'm alive. I am grateful."

No, I hadn't called 911. Calling for help means you are your-self helpless. I did not think that I was helpless and I had not been a victim exactly. *Not raped, not strangled. Alive.*

It filled me with revulsion, the thought of calling Princeton police to Charter Street. To this shabbily elegant old Victorian house at 28 Charter Street where mostly single residents lived, and all of us associated with the university in some way. It filled me with revulsion to consider identifying myself as yet another female victim of masculine violence.

I knew how the inquiry would proceed. Those years, living with Hedy Quade, I came to know plenty. She'd had "incidents" with men also and the first thing the police ask is, Did you know your assailant, and the second thing they ask is, Did you let him voluntarily into your living quarters.

In fact I had not been raped, and I had not been strangled, and I hadn't been assaulted brutally, and I wasn't sure if I had even been threatened. This was a matter of pride: my pride. I could take care of myself.

It seemed to me unlikely that Zedrick Dewe would return. I could not believe that I meant much to him. I understood that, from his perspective, I had led him on. I'd been drinking, and my usual reserve had melted. My usual vigilance had melted. He'd called me a cocktease, he'd accused me of thinking I was too good for him. I was not a feminist who believes that a woman can befriend a man—sexually entice a man—and then reject him without consequences.

Since childhood I was not one to believe that anything we do is without consequences, for which we must accept responsibility.

It was an accident, no one died.

It was an accident, that no one died.

The morning after. Downstairs, in the vestibule of the house.

Where I stood staring at the row of mailboxes. Eight tenants lived at 28 Charter Street of whom one had neatly identified herself as *L. Quade, 2 C.* My heart pounded, I saw something inside the mailbox that could not be mail for mail isn't delivered so early. Yet I could not bring myself to unlock the box.

"Miss Quade? Good morning."

The raspy smoker's voice of my downstairs neighbor. She was a brisk white-haired reference librarian at the university whose demeanor with me was usually cordial but, this morning, she was clearly annoyed.

"Miss Quade! It sounded like a drunken brawl in your apartment last night but it couldn't have been a drunken brawl, I'm sure."

I could think of no reply. A wave of shame passed over me.

"Your gentleman friend has a loud voice. And very heavy feet."

I murmured that I was sorry, it wouldn't happen again.

"I hope not, Miss Quade. 'Again'—and your neighbors will be calling the police."

I was desperate to avoid this aggressive woman but she followed me outside. The bright air of morning, after my miserable sleepless night, struck the top of my head like a fist.

Yet how peaceful Charter Street was at this hour. A quarter-mile hill, comprised of old but neatly maintained wood frame houses built close to the sidewalk. The façades of those houses facing east—white, pale yellow, pale green—shone with reflected sunlight like the façades of houses in certain paintings of Edward Hopper.

In the bright light, my swollen lip and the bruise above my left eye must have been more visible, for my white-haired neighbor broke off her complaint to stare at me, and spoke then with concern, "Lara, did someone—your visitor last night—hurt you?"

I was glancing nervously up and down the street, which was narrow and one way; residents of Charter Street had no driveways, and parked their cars at the curb; I saw with a shock how easy it would be for someone to crouch behind one of those cars, waiting to confront an unwary pedestrian.

"No. Thank you. I'm—fine."

I was rudely abrupt. I was desperate to escape. I would walk quickly up Charter Street in the middle of the street, so long as there was no traffic. My white-haired neighbor had more to say to me, might even have placed a comforting hand on my arm, but I turned away.

It was no note from Zedrick Dewe in my mailbox, as I discovered that evening. Instead, a voucher from a local pizzeria.

• • •

He won't be back. He despises you.

At the Institute I made inquiries among the staff. I asked the director's private secretary. I went to Richardson Auditorium to ask at the box office. Just to explain what I wanted to know made me anxious. I heard myself stammer: "A ticket for the concert on April 23—my seat was C 22—I'm wondering if you have any record, who might have purchased this ticket? It came to me in the mail anonymously."

No one could help me. The request was so trivial. The director's secretary told me, yes the Institute bought block tickets to concert and theater series, and if these tickets weren't all used some were passed out to students, but not individually, and not anonymously. I showed her the envelope with *L Quade* written on it and she shook her head, bemused.

"Sorry, Lara. That isn't ours. It isn't the director's policy to do anything anonymously."

Metuchen, he said. An hour's drive. Not far.

Four. Five. Six days after.

The little half-empty box of matches I'd taken from Zedrick Dewe's jacket pocket and hidden away in a desk drawer. I had not yet opened that drawer.

•   •   •

I told no one. I would tell no one.

Reasoning *Look: he won't be back. You're safe.*

Though hearing Momma's murmurous seductive voice of long ago *He's hunting us. Wants to hurt us. He has cast his lot with the devil.*

His mother had been killed, he'd said. Murdered.

Back in the early 1970s. Where, he hadn't said.

My immediate reaction had been to reach out to him, to touch his arm. But I had not. In fact I had shivered, with a purely visceral reaction.

I tried to recall what Zedrick Dewe had said about his mother. She was oddly named—"Jonquil." He'd spoken of her with an air of pain, disapproval. *I'd have been home, I'd have been killed, too. With the same knife.*

I was not haunted by Zedrick Dewe. I don't think so. Though I was wary of his presence. I mean, I kept my door locked at all times. My windows locked, shades drawn. Even during the day. I took no chances. *A young woman living alone, object of a possible stalker, must take no chances.*

I knew: Zedrick Dewe was not stalking me. I knew.

Seven days after. And I had not glimpsed him on Charter Street or Nassau Street or in the vicinity of the Institute. And I had not received any message from him. Any threatening telephone call.

Yet each time I stepped outside the house at 28 Charter, and each time I returned, I was nearly overcome by anxiety. Blinking rapidly to clear moisture from my eyes so that I could see my assailant before he struck. Often on the stairs I heard his low sneering voice close beside me. As I fumbled to unlock my door. *Lorraine?*

I could not comprehend why, why he'd called me by that name several times. Had it been drunken carelessness, or had it meant something?

Your own fault. You didn't need to tell him you'd ever been 'Lorraine.'

Yet I was practical-minded, I think. Avoiding deserted streets. Walking alone at night in well-lighted places only. At the Institute, making an effort to be cheerful, upbeat, articulate, "intellectual"; making an effort not to reveal weakness, anxiety. If your hand shakes, steady it. If your voice shakes, take a deep breath and calm down.

If someone comes up behind you as you're working at a computer, resist the impulse to recoil in panic. Resist the impulse to scream.

Telling myself *Look: he won't be back* yet I could not remain in my apartment unless I barricaded the door. Cleverly positioning a low-backed chair in front of the door, back fitted securely beneath the doorknob.

Not answering my telephone. Letting the calls, which were not frequent, record on the answering machine.

Nights were difficult. Nights were hell. I did not believe in sleeping pills, and I knew better than to drink. *A single glass of wine won't hurt. One or two glasses. Just to sleep.*

No. Hedy Quade was my example, I knew better.

Duncan Quade. Kicking a chair across the kitchen, shoving Momma against the wall. Grabbing Ryan and me, squeezing us so tight he nearly broke our ribs, protesting how he loved us, loved his kids, just couldn't live with us any longer.

Ryan Quade, my junkie brother. Expelled from junior high school for chronic drunkenness. Aged thirteen.

Sleep! Since the assault it was becoming ever more elusive like a cloud of shimmering light you reach for, and reach through—grasping nothing.

Lonely people crave sleep. Since the car crash of my childhood I had craved sleep. Because sleep is the refuge, the escape. Sleep is a way of slipping from the self, yet not erasing the self altogether.

Sleep it off Momma used to say.

Momma had liked to sleep more and more, those last years before I ran away. Drinking herself to sleep in bed so that one of us, Ryan or me, usually me, had to remove her burning cigarette from her fingers. But we hardly dared touch Momma because that would awaken her and she'd be confused and remorseful, saying what a bad mother she was, and she hadn't ever meant to be bad in any way, or worse yet she'd be furious with us, swiping clumsily at us with her fists. And we didn't dare switch off the bedside lamp because darkness scared Momma, woke her like a slap in the face.

My strategy was: work late at the Institute, come home and

work more until I was too exhausted to see straight. Then I would lie on my bed without removing most of my clothes. Telling myself I was just resting my eyes. This wasn't a serious attempt at sleep, don't be anxious if you can't sleep.

Of course, I left lights on, too.

And the door barricaded.

Zed. A name for Nothing. A name for Nought.

Sprawling exhausted in a sandy beach. A littered beach, at Lake Ontario. Sleep was the thin hissing surf washing over me, my helpless body. Sleep like a caress. Yet the surf sucked away sand beneath me. Small sucking mouths. So that I stirred fretfully, I whimpered in my sleep, woke tasting grit, the residue of Irish whiskey and a man's saliva.

The man himself hunched over me. Gripping my face in his hand.

Cocktease, cunt. Lorraine.

In desperation I tried to draw breath to scream, but could not scream.

But I love you. Wanted to love you.

Above my bed, a shelf of dolls.

At the age of twenty-eight, I did not sleep with dolls. Though in my confused dreams sometimes I was a little girl clutching at Bessie.

Still it seemed unfair to me, that Bessie had been taken from me.

And now, poor Tina. She was a cheap doll and yet a very pretty doll of a kind no longer manufactured. Our assailant had broken her neck, and I'd tried to mend her. Whenever I glanced at her, it seemed to me that her face was frozen into an expression of startled incredulity.

Why do you hate me? Why would you want to hurt—me?

For the grief of my loss I had, as always, work.

Back in elementary school I'd learned to depend upon work.

And so I worked. I worked at the Institute, and I worked at the university library, and I worked at home.

And I kept things clean. Always, after having been Hedy Quade's daughter for sixteen years, I kept things clean.

I vacuumed the apartment. I scrubbed. The apartment he'd despoiled had to be reclaimed as my own. The bright patterned fabrics, the broken chair and broken lamp and whiskey-stained rug. All those things Zedrick Dewe had struck in his fury, I returned to their rightful positions; what wasn't mendable, I threw away. In my braided rug the whiskey stain wasn't visible but the sickly sweet smell lingered.

Eventually I would buy another rug, I supposed. Eventually, I would have to move.

• • •

"All events are accidents. You can argue this."

"All 'cataclysmic' events are contingent events."

"The very concept of 'accident'—"

"Assaults. Murders. Mass murder. The phenomenon we designate as 'war'—to distinguish from 'mere murder.' "

"You can argue, yes all events are 'accidents.' But assaults of human beings by other human beings are willed, and volitional; they may be premeditated; assaults are not 'acts of God' that no human agency can forestall."

" 'Accident' and 'necessity'—"

"These are linguistic conventions merely. As Wittgenstein saw, there are no philosophical problems, only just problems of language. And these are outmoded in the twenty-first century. For, from Spinoza's perspective, all things are of necessity, while, from a post-Heisenberg perspective—"

"All things are contingent, chance."

"No! As Einstein says, 'God does not play dice with the universe.' "

"But God does play dice with the universe. Post-Heisenberg—"

"You are in the wrong place at the wrong time, it's a temporal/spatial accident. No more. Or, rather, you are in the 'right' place at the 'right' time—"

"It comes to the same thing."

"Not exactly. If one of the contingencies is—"

Early May. A three-day symposium at the Institute. Visiting lecturers and panelists from the most distinguished universities. Fellows were meant to participate but did very little speaking, of course.

"Miss Quade! A younger perspective. Tell us what you think, Lara."

I laughed. I walked out.

Now sometimes the telephone rang, and I saw my hand reach out to lift the receiver, and my hand froze before touching the receiver, and when I checked the answering machine there was nothing.

Not even a murmur of derision as he hung up the phone.

Fuck you, Lorraine.

Strange, the things a research fellow discovers.

Like an archeological dig, my work. Like leafing through the brittle pages of a very old photo album in which everyone pictured is now vanished.

For instance: there were humanoid dolls of the nineteenth century which were equipped with crude mechanical "voices"; in some cases these voices issued from artificial mouths that included teeth and gums. The talking dolls were often life-sized and always female—Euphonia, Minerva, Pandora, Serena. These were precursors of the phonograph to be invented by Thomas Edison in the late 1870s. It was Edison's great dream to preserve the dead by recording voices before death and inserting recordings into doll-replicas of the deceased, in this way providing mankind a kind of "immortality."

Such discoveries filled me with a profound melancholy. I wanted to cry. Though better to laugh.

• • •

You would be surprised, I laughed often in those days.

Thinking *My doll-life. He has smashed it.*

With a careless sweep of his ropey-muscled arm. With care-less contemptuous words.

I was desperate to regain my doll-life but had forgotten how I'd lived then, only a few days ago.

8

---

7 May 1993:
Institute for Semiotics,
Aesthetics, and
Cultural Research,
Princeton, New Jersey

LARA QUADE:

Your report on the "talking dolls" is most intriguing. A return to your first-rate work of last fall. Please expand considerably & provide exact sources incl. photographs wherever possible & facsimiles of original newspaper accounts. Equally crucial, all of Edison's commentary & relevant correspondence.

This, an e-mail from the Director of the Institute, who rarely communicated with his research assistants in so enthusiastic and personal a tone. I was astonished, and read and reread the message on my computer screen, my eyes filling with tears. It was the closest to an affectionate caress I had had in memory.

A doll has no feelings. No need to cry even when she's been

kicked between the legs (for there is nothing between a doll's legs) and her neck and head broken. But a living woman requires so much more.

"He can help me. He will protect me."

I whispered these words aloud. I seemed to believe this though I couldn't have said exactly in what way the Director of the Institute of Semiotics, Aesthetics, and Cultural Studies whom I scarcely knew could protect me. (From whom, and from what?) I was completing my first academic term as an Institute fellow on a two-year contract, and beyond the following year my future was as hazy as mist above a void.

My future as hazy as my past.

"Lara Quade? The Director wishes to see you."

At last the summons came. I was suffused with hope like a blinding flash of light.

It had been eighteen days since the evening of the Japanese pianist, and the early-morning assault in my apartment.

During these days I had not seen Zedrick Dewe and was convinced that he wasn't stalking me even as I felt his thoughts obsessively fixed upon me. *Can't forget. There is a bond between us.* In my apartment on Charter Street which I'd once liked so very much and now disliked, the man's scent prevailed: oiled hair, sweetish-stale sweat, whiskey, masculine outrage. When I unlocked the door, my heart pounded in wariness: *Don't enter! He's here.* I felt the vibration of his footsteps. I felt the quivering of the air as he moved through it. I felt the impress of his hands on my shoulders, his hard hungry mouth against mine, grinding against my teeth. In my twilit bedroom the forlorn grouping of dolls gazed down upon my bed where you could see, from a certain angle, the impress of a man's body on the quilt coverlet. A scent of his hair on the pillow.

I shook my head, to wake myself from a trance.

Yet in the street I sometimes heard *Lor-raine! Doll-Lara!* in a jeering caress. In the buzz of voices in public places and sometimes even, to my chagrin, at the Institute. I heard, and was paralyzed with fear. More than once, walking with colleagues from the Institute, I happened to glance up to see on Nassau Street or on Washington Road a suspicious vehicle moving past: a battered minivan driven by a tall lanky figure with straggly hair.

Stalking me like a hunter, he will never forgive.

Yet at the same time I understood: Zedrick Dewe was gone from Princeton, and wouldn't return. No one was stalking me. No one was thinking obsessively of me.

Still I wasn't able in those days to prepare even simple meals in my apartment. Some days, I avoided eating at all.

For these reasons my eyes shone with a dark hectic glisten like the glisten of madness and my skin was feverish and men glanced at me with interest and so too did the Director's eyes move upon me with interest, surprise and interest, when I entered his airy light-filled office suite on the top floor of the Institute.

Usually the Director's eyes were heavy-lidded as a turtle's, and his gaze somnolent. The Director was a man-mammoth weighing perhaps 320 pounds. His face was a flaccid, sallow, part-collapsed Buddha face occasionally enlivened by a thought.

This morning, the Director appeared alert, even kindly.

"Lara, I have a favor to ask that, I hope, will not inconvenience you."

How like the Director to speak. He was a theorist whose linguistic obscurity rivaled that of Jacques Lacan. Rarely did the Director speak directly, but in code.

The only response to the Director's remark that was required on my part was an obedient expression, possibly a small smile.

Not a vivacious smile. Not a coy or a seductive smile. For all his size, the Director was a subtle man like most intellectuals of his repute and was known to appreciate subtlety in others.

Especially in young-female others.

The Director was a famous man. In certain circles, a celebrity. He was a powerful man: he'd founded the famous Institute himself, and he controlled every appointment from senior faculty to very junior faculty, secretarial staff, and assistants (like me) of whom there were about fifteen. The Director was feared, and revered. The Director was known for small, random, unprovoked acts of both kindness and cruelty: if you were the recipient of his kindness this didn't mean that you would not, one day, be the recipient of his cruelty; but if you were the recipient of cruelty, it did mean that you would never be the recipient of his kindness, for the Director had written you off as of no value to him.

My presence at the Institute was a consequence of the Director's kindness: he'd approved my two-year appointment. It was rumored that only fifteen applicants were accepted out of several hundred applications. At our initial meeting back in September, the Director had smiled sleepily in my direction, and uttered my name—"Lara Quade"—in a thrillingly mellifluous yet somehow questioning voice. I had said, "Yes, sir?" but the Director seemed not to hear, for he hadn't been speaking to me, he'd simply uttered my name as if it were an oddity, a foreign phrase perhaps. Abruptly then he'd turned from me, to speak to another fellow. A few weeks later, he had marked one of my reports *v. satisfactory* and he had invited me to have lunch with him at the University Club; I had been wary of the invitation, for by this time I knew of the Director's reputation for fickleness. You risked professional ruin if you misinterpreted his notoriously subtle signals; still, it was risky to decline an invitation from him, too. In the end, I explained to the Director that I could not take time for lunch, it was my practice to work through the lunch hour; the Director seemed to accept this excuse graciously—"Well, then, Laura! Another time. Perhaps." Since then, the Director had not communicated directly with me and would seem to have forgotten my existence.

"Miss Quade, here is the issue: I need this 'talking doll' material earlier than I'd originally told you. And of course I need detailed footnotes, and slides of the visuals, by next Monday."

Even while seated, the Director breathed through his mouth as if he'd been climbing stairs. On his bald Buddha-head oily perspiration shone, which he dabbed at languidly with a handkerchief. Though overwarm, the Director never loosened his striking silk necktie (Dior? J. Press?), nor did he remove his beautifully English-tailored suit coat, for one of the Director's fetishes was an impeccable public persona. You imagined him sweating through his custom-made silk shirts, hidden beneath his stylish coats.

Next Monday!

My mind worked rapidly as clockwork. *It's Wednesday now. I can't possibly do it.* The Director was scheduled to lecture at Cambridge University, England, sometime the following week. His stylish new project was titled *From Madness to Myth: A Cultural Anatomy of the Uncanny.* I understood that my newly discovered material would be integral to this lecture; from past experience I knew how ingeniously the Director would rework my research into his own language, he would "illuminate" it with one of his controversial theories, and it would be received by his British audience as brilliant, though obscure.

Seeing me hesitate, the Director frowned.

"And the Vaucanson material, I forgot to mention. Very promising but surely you can expand this. More French phrases, please. After all, Vaucanson was French."

Much of this material I had prepared months ago. Other assistants had worked on it in the interim. The Director was publishing his work-in-progress serially; it would run to nearly one thousand pages. Especially the Director was known for his erudite and witty footnotes, which often doubled the length of his chapters. His relationship to his research fellows was roughly that of a Renaissance artist to his apprentices: the Director assigned research subjects, you prepared initial drafts of chapters for him, received from him initial drafts of chapters prepared by other assistants which you were to revise and "expand" as they revised and "expanded" your drafts; after some time, when the drafts were substantial, the Director went through them inserting his signature buzz words—*trope, paradigmatic, analogical, apocalyptic*—and other stylistic quirks unique to the Director. When *From Madness to Myth* was finally published it would include an acknowledgments page graciously thanking the Director's distinguished colleagues and scholar-friends, and of course the Director's wife ("dear incomparable Elizabeth, long-enduring spouse of a workaholic"), but there would be no mention of the Director's research assistants. We were seasonal labor, and expendable. By the time the book was published we would all be vanished from Princeton.

Unless the Director intervened, of course. Unless, in his unpredictably generous way, he chose to protect one of us by renewing her contract for another two years.

The Director was regarding me intently.

"Lara, dear? You won't disappoint me—I hope?"

A sheaf of papers lay on the edge of the Director's handsome blond oak desk. I understood that I was meant to pick it up and so I did, with an unwavering hand.

I assured the Director, yes I would be happy to prepare the material he wanted. I would stay late at the Institute each night until Monday. Allowing him to know *I have no private life, you see. I am yours.*

My quiet words struck the Director like music: like the opening chords of the most dreamy ethereal Debussy, that promises so much. For this rare occasion I was wearing one of my most feminine doll-costumes: long narrow white linen skirt, white-patterned stockings, a boxy-shouldered short-sleeved linen jacket. These were Second-Time-Around purchases, classic high-quality clothes. My glossy black hair spilled about my heart-shaped face, and my face had been carefully painted and powdered to disguise lingering blemishes and insomniac bruises beneath my eyes. From this angle, and at such a distance, the Director would probably not take note of defects at my hairline or beneath my jaw. I think he was most impressed by my manner that was both deferential and efficient, and by the incline of my head that mimicked that of Tina's broken/mended head on her delicate shoulders.

Surprisingly, the Director stood. It was rare to see him heave himself to his feet. His breath was labored and hissing, like the breath through a tracheotomy incision. His fleshy lips moved with unusual zest. "Lara: I have a new idea. Would you accompany me to Cambridge next week, as my assistant? We will fly first-class, and we will stay in first-class hotels in Cambridge and London for six days. Does that appeal to you, my dear? If you finish the material on Monday, of course."

I told the Director, yes the invitation appealed to me, very much.

And, yes I would finish the material on time.

Cocktease. Cunt. Think you're too good for me, huh?

Now I could laugh at Zedrick Dewe. That crude pathetic lout, that swaggering bully.

I foresaw: the Director would be *v. pleased* with me and would hire me as his personal assistant, and I would accompany him everywhere. I foresaw: the Director would fall in love with me, and he would be a gentle, gentlemanly lover (for his massive weight would preclude conventional sex, perhaps all sex, wouldn't it?). I foresaw: the Director would divorce his wife of thirty years and marry me.

All this I dreamt while lying partly dressed across my bed, leafing through the pages of an old, outsized book and staring at plates of daguerreotypes of "Euphonia"—"Minerva"—"Pandora"—"Serena." All this I dreamt lying across my bed in my apartment faintly smelling still of spilled whiskey, a chair propped against the front door to protect me against my assailant.

9

August–September 1970:
Lake Shaheen, New York

Estranged. The first of the words from the summer of my sixth year, and the most beautiful and mysterious. There was Momma wiping at her eyes with the back of her hand explaining to someone over the phone *My husband and I are estranged* so the sound of her words had the melancholy of a country song. For Hedy Quade had dignity then.

Rectify. Another of the mysterious words of that summer. Daddy had come home to talk to Ryan and me outside on the porch, Momma refused to allow him inside, he was saying goodbye and why he couldn't take us to live with him just yet, running his hand roughly over my head making tears spring into my eyes saying it was a time of change, *I made mistakes in my life I have to rectify*.

Betrayal was a new strange word. And *whore*.

Swine we knew. *Bastard, son of a bitch, liar, fucker*. These words we knew, we were hearing often.

•   •   •

When Momma spoke to you, you believed Momma. When Daddy spoke to you, you believed Daddy.

Momma said that Daddy did not love us any longer, Daddy did not want to live with us but had cast his lot with swine. Daddy said that he loved us more than his own life, he loved Momma too but he could not live with us right now for *It would end up one of us killing the other.*

10

—

Christmas 1970:
Lake Shaheen, New York

Attica was another of those mysterious words. But harsh, and not beautiful. *Attica* murmured out of earshot and not for Ryan and me to hear. And so in fact I did not hear it. *Attica Attica* murmured in adult voices of mystery and authority and never to be questioned.

There was Momma in her chenille robe belted so tight around her waist, it looked as if the robe was breathing, panting. And Momma's hand lifting her cigarette to her mouth, trembling.

"Your Daddy won't be seeing you. Not for Christmas. Not for a long time."

Why? we asked.

"Why! There's a reason. So don't let me hear you bawling. Neither of you. Not at Christmas, and not at any time."

Momma, why? we asked.

Momma turned her face aside. She had cut her hair with a scissors in desperation that night, to get the blood out of it, but now her hair was growing long again, streaked with threads of silver like glinting wires. Her mouth that had been red and luscious was pale and soft now, torn like a fish's mouth where the hook has gone in.

"You damn kids. You damn sad pathetic kids. Sure there's a reason! But you're not to know."

Oh Momma, why? we asked.

In his loud whiny voice Ryan demanded to know.

Momma, *why?*

Still Momma's face was turned away. When her mouth moved, you could almost not hear her.

"Because—"

From the living room the TV voices were talking and laughing. The TV was almost always on now, day and night. And Daddy's portable radio in the kitchen. Tuned to the country-music station that was Daddy's and Momma's favorite. If you stood outside you could hear the TV voices and the radio voices and you would think a big family lived in that house, filling up all the rooms.

Momma stood so long staring at some point we couldn't see like it was floating in the air above our heads, and Momma held her hand so stiff not even smoking her cigarette like a store dummy, finally Ryan began giggling, and I backed away shoving all my fingers I could get into my mouth fearful of giggling wild and hurtful in me like sobbing, that would plug up my head and make my eyes blind like Bessie's eyes.

Because! because he is gone! because he did a bad thing! because your daddy is bad! your daddy is locked away with others of his kind who cast their lot with swine.

11

---

14 May 1993:
Princeton, New Jersey

"Lara? Have you heard the terrible news?"

I had not.

"The Director is in the Princeton Medical Center in 'critical condition.' He was mugged last night, and 'savagely beaten.' "

The bearer of this astonishing news was one of the young Institute secretaries. Her voice quivered with dismay.

I stood unmoving. I may have tried to speak. My eyes welled with tears of shock, sympathy. And fear.

I turned and made my way along a corridor, half-blinded. I could hear others speaking of the "mugging": my dazed brain fastened upon the curious word, *mug, mugging,* what extravagant claims the Director made for the vagaries of language, those interstices in which meaning leaps, flashes, reveals itself like silvery fish surfacing in the waves, and then—vanishes.

A *mug* is a face. To be *mugged* is to be—defaced? Effaced?

In the background were more voices. I did not want to hear. "Mugged? How badly?"

". . . 'near death' . . ."

"No! My God! Who . . ."

"The police don't know. They think . . ."

I entered the cubicle-office I shared with two other research assistants, like me protégées of the Director, and sat numbed in front of my computer terminal staring at—what? The screen saver swirling slow and silent, a brainless cycle of falling snow.

His revenge. It can't be. But yes.

It was two days after the Director had summoned me into his airy light-filled office. Two days after I'd made my decision to accompany him to England. The intervening days had been frantic and purposeful: I'd worked every waking minute, zealous, frantic to obey the Director's command, I wanted not only to serve him but to obliterate myself, my emotions, in such service; and I wanted the man to know how I revered him, and did not think of myself. I would have worked in my sleep if I'd been capable. This was a flaw in human beings, requiring sleep, otherwise some of us would be the most devoted of wind-up dolls!

After eighteen hours I'd e-mailed some of my new material to the Director and had received from him a reply so concise, so enigmatic it seemed to me poetry, to be interpreted as a private message in code:

v.v. satisfactory Lara Quade!

A message that so thrilled me, I printed it out and taped it to the blank white wall beside my desk.

It was a state of suspended panic at the Institute. Telephones were ringing, people drifted about in the corridors, unable to work yet unwilling to go home. The Director's personal assistant Martha called me upstairs to tell me, grimly: "Oh Miss Quade! The trip to England is canceled. As you must know."

Martha had been helping to expedite my passport for the trip. For of course I had no passport, I'd never traveled outside the United States. At the Institute, I must have been something of a novelty, a freak: a young academic woman, evidently a valued protégée of the Director's, who had never left the country of her birth. It was like the Director to set his overworked and fanatically loyal assistant to "expedite" my travel plans; I was able to gather, by remarks of Martha's, that another young woman assistant had been scheduled to accompany the Director to England, but now that woman was not going, and I was; this change of plans Martha accepted with a cheerful sort of stoicism, as one more challenge cast at her, into her capable hands, by the great man.

But now the trip had been cancelled. The Director's very life was in danger. Martha stared at me, dabbing at her reddened eyes with a tissue. Hoarsely she said, ". . . such a shock. To us all. And to *you*."

I seemed almost to detect a note of reproach in this remark.

Almost immediately the telephone rang. Martha picked up the receiver eagerly. I was absolved of having to speak. My throat was numb. Through a roaring in my ears I would learn that the

Director was on a respirator, in the intensive care unit of the medical center; he had not yet regained consciousness; his skull was fractured, and numerous bones were broken and sprained. I would learn that his assailant had not been caught, or identified. Police issued a statement that the mugging was believed to have been a "crime of opportunity"—not a personal but an impersonal assault. The mugger had followed his victim into a parking garage off Palmer Square sometime after 11 P.M. when the garage was deserted, he'd attacked the Director as the Director was un- locking his car, hitting him on the back of the skull so hard, with a blunt weapon like a hammer, that the Director had collapsed at once. The lone parking attendant two flights down had heard nothing, and claimed to have seen no one "suspicious" enter the garage all evening.

Here were ugly facts: as the Director lay unconscious and bleeding, his assailant had continued to beat him, breaking his jaw with the blunt weapon, cracking several ribs, kicking his thighs and groin, tearing his clothing and ripping off his necktie, removing his money and credit cards from his wallet which he then tossed down onto the Director's chest.

Contemptuously, you had to suppose. *The (faceless) mugger tossing his victim's empty wallet onto the victim's obese heaving chest.*

I began to cough. I could not stop coughing.

Tears flooded my eyes and spilled onto my cheeks.

Martha saw that I was genuinely stricken, and went quickly to bring me a glass of water. Through my coughing I was trying to ask, "Is he expected to live?"

12

―――

14 May 1993:
Princeton, New Jersey

*H*e *has been here. Someone has been here.*

Even before I entered the living room I could see that there
was something wrong. I could smell his scent.

Visually, viscerally, objects were out of alignment. The windows were narrower than I recalled, and the drawn shades were
shabbier. The floorboards were slanted like the floorboards of
Van Goh's painting of his room. Shadows fell at perverse angles in
no logical relationship to sources of light. Shadows were dispro-
portionate to the objects that cast them.

My dolls! They had been prankishly re-arranged on their
high shelf above rows of books. Tina with her broken/mended
curly-black head and parted rosebud lips had been re-
positioned. Her shiny white satin bridal gown was more wrinkled
and soiled than it had been that morning, as if someone had
crushed her in his grimy fist.

And the smell: as of singed hair, oiled hair. A stale odor of
male perspiration.

"You have no right to do this! I'll call the police . . ."

I spoke in a lowered desperate voice. I would not have wanted my downstairs neighbor to hear me talking to myself like a deranged woman.

Obviously, the intruder was gone now. He had re-locked the door, almost you wouldn't know it had been forced open.

I switched on all the lights in the living room, as if reclaiming that room, then I moved on cautiously to the tiny kitchen alcove, where I saw at once that one of the glasses, which I kept sparkling clean on the windowsill above the sink, had been used. He'd drunk from it, the impress of his mouth on the rim glowed with a just-visible scummy phosphorescence.

"Damn you! Disgusting."

I was reminded of my brother, long ago. Not Ryan in his druggie-meanness as he'd been during the last few months we'd lived in the same house in Phoenix, but Ryan when he'd been younger, ten, eleven years old, a boy who was fond of his younger sister, I suppose, but couldn't resist teasing and torment-ing me, making a mess of my carefully sorted possessions. My dolls, my glass animals. Cheap dime store purchases that had meant so much to me in my childish loneliness . . .

Quickly I washed the glass at the faucet. Washed and dried it and replaced it on the windowsill.

I dreaded checking my bedroom. My bathroom.

It had been an exhausting day. After learning of the Director's condition I could not work in my office at the Institute: no one at the Institute was behaving normally, the mood was stricken and anarchic. If he dies? What will happen to us? Our fears were unwarranted: the Institute would be headed by another Director, of course. The Institute was a self-sustaining institution, richly endowed. Yet I felt this dismay, this despair. For the Director had singled me out for an act of kindness; he had singled me out for a privileged fate; and now that had been taken from me.

I didn't want to think by whom. And why.

Bulletins from the medical center came hourly—" 'His condition is unchanged.' "

I went to the university library, but could not concentrate there, either. My research into automata that had fascinated me for months was beginning now to sicken me. Dolls—talking dolls—humanoids—"automata": I would have liked to smash these monstrosities if I'd been able.

Those eighteenth- and nineteenth-century automata that still existed, in museums and private collections, were worth hundreds of thousands of dollars. These especially I'd have liked to smash with a sledgehammer.

I hadn't wanted to come back to this apartment. I'd left the library and walked to the Princeton Medical Center, a high-rise building on Witherspoon Street. Never before had I been in the Medical Center, and as soon as I entered I recalled Port Oriskany General Hospital where as a child I'd been a patient recovering from the "trauma" of a car crash. Where the air-conditioning was so cold, the smells of sickness and disinfectant so strong.

Will he—live? This was the question anxiously asked about my brother Ryan. Of the three of us in the mangled car, Ryan was the most seriously injured. He too had been in intensive care and on a respirator; among his injuries was a skull concussion, pinpoint hemorrhages causing the brain to swell.

Ryan had been in a coma for six days. Then he'd awakened, and revived. After twenty-one days, he was discharged from the hospital into the care of his mother, Mrs. Duncan Quade.

In the Medical Center I'd walked about slowly as if underwater. Weights dragging at my ankles.

Three times I inquired after the Director at the information desk and three times I was told politely that the Director's condition "remained stable."

"But do the doctors think he will—live?"

(Almost, I'd said *die*.)

The woman at the information desk, a volunteer, frowned at me as if I'd said something obscene.

I knew she couldn't help me with such a question. But I asked, in child-like desperation I asked, for it seemed required of me.

Look, he isn't coming back: he despises you.

He knows nothing of the Institute, the Director. He can't have done this thing.

As soon as I stepped into my bedroom, I knew he'd been here.

For here his scent was stronger, like an animal's.

I checked the bathroom: no one was behind the door.

I saw that the toilet was unflushed: yellow with urine.

Quickly I flushed it, and backed away.

"Pig. Disgusting."

I drew my fingers across the coverlet on my bed. I could see that he'd lain here. I could make out the impress of his body, a man's heavy insolent body, on the bed. Dirty work boots, oiled hair. That ridiculous hair! I was sickened to think that he might have flung back the covers, and lain in my sheets to contaminate them.

"Bastard. Utter . . ."

Suddenly, I knew: I yanked open the top drawer of my bureau, and saw that someone had been rummaging in this drawer, and that my father's watch was gone.

"Oh God. No."

This was the cruel blow. This was the kick between the legs.

This was the man's revenge, for he'd seen how much the watch meant to me. When I'd taken it out to show him (why the hell had I showed my father's watch to that man, a stranger? had I been crazy?) he'd seen. Gazing at me with his glistening eyes.

I had invited this. I had been boastful. Showing the watch as if claiming *I had a father once. He is gone now but I had him, once.*

I groped for the missing watch in the drawer, tossing aside my stockings, underwear, velvet headbands. All the corners of the shallow drawer where obviously it was not.

I yanked out the other drawers. Desperate, panicked. Crying. Cursing. In the bottom drawer was the cream-colored envelope with *L Quade* written on it, which Zedrick Dewe must have placed here for some taunting purpose.

Why? I could not imagine.

I was squatting on my heels in front of the bureau. I'd yanked out the drawers, that had nearly fallen onto me. It was a fact, Zedrick Dewe had broken into my apartment; all these days and nights I'd been deluding myself, that my fears of him were un-grounded, only just female paranoia. *He is real, he has been here. He is stalking you.*

Then I saw that the envelope wasn't the old one, but a new one.

How could this be? I could not comprehend.

The original envelope had had a typed address beneath my name but this envelope had only

L Quade

on its front.

Had Zedrick Dewe made out the first envelope, too? To *L Quade*?

Not an anonymous Princeton benefactor but—Zedrick Dewe, of Metuchen, New Jersey?

I saw that something bulky had been stuffed inside this envelope and when I opened the envelope with shaking fingers and pulled it out it was a—necktie.

An expensive silk tie stiff with bloodstains. A very dark blue with almost imperceptible dark stripes, I had last seen on the Director.

13

9 April 1971:
Lake Shaheen, New York

Are we going to see Daddy? Where is Daddy?
Momma? Where is Daddy?

News had come to Momma over the phone. At about 9 A.M. of that day. We heard her in the kitchen stumbling to answer the ringing phone, it was a morning when Momma must have felt hopeful, for her voice lifted light as a girl's, "Yes?" It was not that day earlier in the week when Momma wore her nightgown and chenille robe through the daytime and lay on the sofa watching TV and drinking and she'd fallen asleep in the stained chenille robe that had been such a fuzzy-soft peach-colored robe when she'd lifted it from a box at Christmas a long time ago I could barely remember, Momma was ashamed of herself she said and not to tell anybody *how low I have fallen* for Hedy Quade too had *cast my lot with swine and God has forsaken me.* It was not that day but a later time, and there came the ringing phone, and after a moment Momma's quick rising voice, "Oh! Oh, God." And the receiver slipped from her hand to thud against the linoleum floor dangling at the end of its rubber cord until Ryan came cautiously to place it back on the wall, and by this time Momma was crying in hoarse ugly gulps like no pretty woman or girl ever cried on TV, hunched on a kitchen chair as a man might sit, her bare white knees exposed and her elbows jammed into her knees, Momma was hiding her face in her hands and sobbing and we backed away knowing not to interrupt her in such grief, whatever her grief was, not to come too near, as you would not reach out to touch, still less to comfort, a wounded feral cat whimpering in pain.

"Momma? Is it Daddy? Did something happen to Daddy?"

"Momma—?"

Daddy had been gone for so long. Since last August Daddy had been gone from us. Momma would not speak of him when we asked where he was or why he would not see us, and Momma's family would not speak of him except to say *Your father is gone from your lives, be grateful.*

Yet all the words that Momma uttered were a way of speaking of our father though she would not utter his name.

On the telephone sometimes speaking stiffly she would say *That man is no longer my husband. Call the Quades if you want news of their son, please don't call this number again.*

Or Momma would shout into the phone *I can't help you. Go to hell!*

We could not leave Momma for very long, to play outdoors. Momma kept us from school saying we were sick with Asian flu and "contagious." Momma kept us from school saying lies were told of her in Lake Shaheen and she would not wish to subject her innocent son and daughter to such lies. We had been told by

Momma that our father was the danger to us, but Ryan said it wasn't Daddy, it was Momma. He would not believe her any longer he said. That Daddy hated us, and wanted to hurt us. Ryan ceased to believe the things that Momma told us but I knew that what Momma told us was *For you kids' own good.*

Another time the telephone rang, but Momma made no move to answer it. Warning us, "Don't either of you two touch that phone, no more than if it's a rattlesnake." So we let it ring, and when it ceased ringing Momma removed it from the hook. She was slow and dazed and her skin was lard-colored.

Later that day Momma would rouse herself. In the late afternoon Momma would wash her face, and change out of her nightgown and robe. Momma would drag a brush through her matted hair. Ryan and me, she dressed without troubling to bathe us. We had not brushed our teeth for two or three days, but Momma paid no heed. Her fingers fumbled our buttons and zippers like the fingers of a blind woman. My snarled hair Momma said she could weep over, but would not—"The time for weeping is past. Cast your lot with the swine of the world, even Jesus will forsake you."

Since Daddy had moved out, Momma watched religion shows on TV a lot. Momma ceased taking us to church but there were TV preachers she favored. Most nights, Momma fell asleep with the TV on.

Momma said, "Be a sweetheart, Ryan. Fetch me your and your sister's jackets." Like Momma was saving her strength, there in the kitchen smiling at us.

It was the first time Momma had smiled at us in a long time. Or called one of us sweetheart.

"You kids, you know your mother loves you. And God loves you. That's all you need to know."

Momma checked the time on the kitchen clock, where you almost couldn't see the numerals because the glass was so splattered with grease. Momma said, "Five-fifteen. That's a time of the day too late to do anything and too early to go to bed."

But five-fifteen was a good time, Momma seemed to think. Almost it seemed she had made a decision, and was smiling now.

Momma put our jackets on but didn't bother with anything for our heads. We'd just be in the car, Momma said.

I wished I had Bessie to take with me. Bessie had disappeared only a few days before.

Daddy's broken watch, I had hidden beneath an edge of the rug in my room. In a corner where no one would step on it. Maybe Ryan knew it was there but he did not tease me or tell Momma on me, or steal it. Maybe like me Ryan checked Daddy's watch to see if it was still there. Slid it onto his wrist smiling to see how big it was, a grown-up man's watch.

Momma hurried us out to the car. Momma was smiling and humming to herself.

"See the sun? The sun is God's big eye."

All that day it had been sleeting and raining but at last the wind had blown the sky clear. There on the far side of the lake was the sun looking red and soft-melting into the foothills. There was no one else on the Shaheen Pike except a neighbor's pickup headed in the opposite direction from us, into the hills. The driver tapped his horn at Momma but Momma did not seem to notice.

I was in the backseat, alone. I wanted to sit in front with

Momma and Ryan but Momma said Oh no, she didn't want us kids causing a ruckus.

It was coming on to dusk. Ryan said for Momma to switch on her headlights but Momma ignored him. For now she was singing softly.

"Rock of Ages cleft for me
Let me hide myself in thee
Let the water and the blood
That from thy wounded side doth flow . . ."

On the Shaheen Pike through the woods. On the curving Shaheen Pike that was route 39. And now descending the long hill toward the town, and the lake. Through the trees you could see the lake glittering in patches like a broken mirror. Lake Shaheen was six miles long but only a mile wide. But as we descended the hill, the lake disappeared into the trees. *Evergreens* these trees were called which I thought was a beautiful word like music.

There was the depot, and there was Texas Hots. There was a train coming fast along the track. Ryan said, "Can we stop at Texas Hots, Momma? Can we?"

He would say he'd heard the crash but had not seen it. He would say he'd been at the back of the café, not looking out the window. He would swear he was not a witness. Hadn't seen a thing so help him God.

II

14

12 May 1993: Princeton, New Jersey

In my desk drawer I found the matchbox printed with:

Otto's White Horse Tavern
Olcott, N.Y.

For a long moment I stared at the address. Olcott was in upstate New York, on Lake Ontario. Less than one hundred miles from Lake Shaheen.

—

15

16–17 May 1993:
Lake Shaheen, New York

You must never go back our mother warned us. *It's a terrible place. Something terrible will happen to you if you go back.*

But I went back. To Lake Shaheen. I seemed to know, it was time for me to return. After twenty-two years.

The first surprise was the small size of the town: Lake Shaheen that had seemed so big to me as a child was no more than a village at the southern end of the lake. In the summer, the population of Lake Shaheen would double, but in the off-season it was probably less than one thousand inhabitants, clustered in a few paved and unpaved streets of small stores, lakeside bungalows and cabins and mobile homes. Along route 41 which led to Lake Shaheen from the east, which I'd taken after exiting the New York Thruway, was the usual dispiriting strip of gas stations and fast-food restaurants, car and mobile home dealerships, mini-malls, hunting and fishing supply stores, bait shops. Most of this was new since Momma had moved us so abruptly away, I supposed. Route 41 had been a country highway. Beyond the highway were the Chautauqua foothills dense with trees as ever, impenetrable. And beyond the foothills, the Chautauqua Mountains.

Living at the base of these mountains, as a child, I never saw them. No one ever did. We "saw" densely wooded slopes, that was all. The Chautauquas were at our back, and we faced front: the Shaheen Pike, leading to town. That five miles to town had seemed a very long distance.

I would not drive past our old house, I thought. I had promised to spare myself.

After Zedrick Dewe, I was going to be cautious. I'd promised myself that, too.

The state highway led into the main street of Lake Shaheen, parallel with the lake. This street of desultory, diminished storefronts where I recognized nothing. But there was the old Anchor Inn Tavern with its open deck above the lake: on Sundays in summer our parents had brought Ryan and me there, in the late afternoon. A smile tugged at my mouth as if this might be a happy memory.

He'd taken us out onto the lake in rowboats. Sometimes Momma came along. *C'mon you kids! All aboard!* Once, Daddy had tried a small sailboat but that hadn't worked so well. Daddy knew nothing about sailboats, and Daddy had been drinking, and Momma kept saying *Oh this wind, this damn wind, why doesn't this wind come straight?*

I'd driven through town and was in a scrubby neighborhood of small wood frame bungalows and cabins on sandy, unpaved

roads leading to the lake; the lake, visible close by, looked diminished, too. In a rutted driveway I turned my car awkwardly
around and drove back on Main Street past the Lake Shaheen
Community & Senior Center, the Lake Shaheen Police, the Lake
Shaheen Post Office, and the Lake Shaheen Public Library in a
quaint cobblestone building smaller than the McDonald's out on
the highway. The library looked familiar, I thought.

You want to remember. You want to have been born somewhere.

There!—my heart leapt to see the white shingleboard
Methodist church with a spire cross shining like tin, where,
sometimes, Mommy had taken Ryan and me. The last few
months, Momma hadn't gone out to church; Momma hadn't gone
out much at all.

Yet sometimes singing under her breath the utterly simple
nursery tune to comfort herself *Jesus loves me this this I know! For
the Bible tells me so.*

Little Lorraine had been so silly: solemnly telling her kindergarten teacher that "Jesus" was a friend of her Momma's. That
"Jesus" came to their house sometimes. Yes he did!

I was passing the elementary school where I'd gone, half-days
to kindergarten for a few months. Ryan had been in fourth grade
at the time of the crash.

Of course, we'd never gone back.

Our mother's zigzag course west and south across the United
States had been necessary to elude pursuers: this was Momma's
fervent belief. Unfortunately it hadn't allowed Ryan and me to go
to school. Not until Poplar Bluffs, Missouri, almost a year after
we'd left Lake Shaheen, where Momma decided at last we could
stop for a while.

God has sent a sign, we'll be safe here.

Thinking of these things I'd been driving blindly. Mailbox after mailbox flashing past and no name meant anything to me.

Never go back there. Something terrible will happen to you.

I was going to drive to Olcott, too. I meant to retrieve my father's watch.

I'd left Princeton abruptly. I had not said when I might be back. The Director was still hospitalized, though no longer in intensive care; it was said of him at the Institute in cautiously optimistic tones that he *would live.*

So, Zedrick Dewe hadn't committed manslaughter, or murder.

I'd gone to look for Zedrick Dewe in Metuchen, New Jersey. I wanted my father's watch back. There was no *Dewe, Zedrick* listed in the Metuchen directory and there was no *Dewe, Zedrick* or any individual resembling him employed by any photo lab in the vicinity and so I was made to see that this stranger had intruded in my life as he'd intruded into my apartment, he'd been stalking me before I was aware of him, sending me the ticket for the concert so that we would be seated together, and we would meet. *Your anonymous benefactor! A stalker, a psychopath.* My heart beat in fury and disgust that I'd been manipulated in such a way. In my ignorance I had invited a dangerous man into my apartment, I might have become his lover that night. Like the Director, I might have been his victim.

Yet I hadn't reported the bloodstained necktie to the police. The cream-colored envelope with the mock-elegant *L Quade.* I had left Princeton instead, like a fugitive.

Driving now along the western shore of Lake Shaheen. All

this was new to me. A child has no sense of geography, I'd formed no sense of the area. "Lake Shaheen"—this name I'd spoken aloud, that had seemed so beautiful and mysterious to me. And perhaps it was beautiful, or had been before the area had become developed. Now I was passing a condominium village, an enclave of stylish A-frame redwood and glass houses, tri-level houses on wooded lots with private docks. But this relatively affluent neighborhood ended abruptly at the junction with route 41. Here was a shabby commercial strip—a lumber yard, a discount shoe store, a garish ten-foot plaster brown bear on its hind legs beside the highway holding aloft a sign:

BEAR ISLE MOBILE VILLAGE

VACANCIES!

A half-mile beyond the mobile village was another sign—
QUADE GAS & AUTO REPAIR.

Quade. My own name came flying at me like a gunshot.

Weakly I thought *Not yet. I am not ready, yet.*

Still, I stopped. On the shoulder of the highway I stopped, and backed my car into the driveway. It was a small family-run garage with only two gas pumps. I maneuvered my car to one of them and asked for gas, a fair-skinned big-bellied man in his mid-forties waited on me, silent, though not unfriendly, taking time to clean my bug-splattered windshield as I tried not to stare avidly at him through the glass. This man: a Quade: a relative of my father's? A cousin, possibly a—brother? My heart was pounding so hard, I could barely stammer out to him, as I paid him for the gas, "My name is 'Quade,' too," as if this were a coincidence to be noted; and the fair-skinned man smiled, startled, squinting at me as if trying to decode me. For this drive of several hundred miles into upstate New York I was wearing jeans, a pullover shirt, a baseball cap. My curly black doll-hair was brushed back from my face and if scar tissue showed, it showed. Inside the loose-fitting shirt my breasts were indiscernible from folds in the material. I wasn't impersonating a guy but I had no intention of impersonating a doll-girl, either.

The fair-skinned man leaned into my window. I saw that his eyes were amber and I wondered if my father's eyes had been that color, too. " 'Quade,' no kidding? Where from?"

"Here."

The fair-skinned man continued to smile at me, puzzled. His eyes had begun to crinkle at the corners in suspicion. "*Here?* Lake Shaheen?"

"My father's name is Duncan Quade."

Not *was.* I couldn't bring myself to say *was.*

Now the fair-skinned man's eyes narrowed. He'd ceased smiling. I understood that "Duncan Quade" meant something to him, and that this meaning was not one he cared to acknowledge.

He said, preoccupied with changing my twenty-dollar bill, not looking at me now, "All that side of the family died out, or moved away."

"You didn't know my father?"

"No."

"You're not—related somehow?"

The fair-skinned man shrugged ambiguously. His face was

shutting up tight and mean as a fist. *Like Daddy. A man like Daddy.* With such a man it was hopeless to plead. Above all it was hopeless to argue.

I asked a few more questions. I was trying not to show that I'd been rebuffed, as we feign ignorance at times in order to disguise our helplessness and dismay. But my Quade relative—for certainly he was this—was impatient to wait on another customer, and backed away. "O.K., miss. Have a great day. Thanks."

So quickly! Our conversation had ended so quickly!

I had no choice but to start the ignition, and drive blindly on.

Consoling myself *Maybe it's true. The simplest truth. All that side of my father's family died, or moved away.*

I'd promised myself that I would not drive by the old house. But I drove by the old house.

Like an alcoholic who knows he must not swallow a mouthful of alcohol, or he will succumb at once, and in a delirium of happiness, to the forbidden, I found myself driving north on route 39. It was my intention to drive only for a few miles, to see how the landscape had changed (or hadn't changed, much) then to turn around and re-enter Lake Shaheen; but I continued driving until I saw the old, suddenly familiar landmarks, a neighbor's barn, a two-acre pasture by the road in which horses had grazed, now overgrown with weeds, and, so suddenly, my parents' house: small, what's called a bungalow, with new asphalt siding simulating beige brick, and bright yellow shutters. The house was set back from the road in a neatly mown lawn. It was still early in the season in the Chautauquas, many of the deciduous trees hadn't their leaves yet, so the place was bright with sunshine, as if over-exposed. I saw that more recent owners had added a carport; someone owned an outboard motorboat; the driveway that had been dirt in my parents' time was now chips of pale gravel. I had to suppose that the interior had been totally remodeled, "modernized." That, if I knocked at the door and asked to be invited in, I would recognize nothing.

I wondered that I felt so little emotion. Like a deaf mute, just staring.

You kids, you know your mother loves you. And God loves you.

I turned in the driveway, and drove back to Lake Shaheen.

A country highway, not commercial like route 41 but mostly woods, a few houses, small farms. The long curving descent to Lake Shaheen I began to feel like a premonition of disaster. Like warning music in a suspense film. As I descended the hill, I saw the highway ahead intersect with the railroad tracks; I passed the sign LAKE SHAHEEN POP. 900. I saw that the railway crossing had gates now, and warning lights. I wondered if these safety features had been there twenty-two years ago. Approaching the intersection I prepared myself for the shock of a train rushing at me but there was nothing.

The railroad bed was raised, like an exposed nerve. Its cinder sides were weedy and littered. I saw to my disappointment that the depot was boarded up and defaced with graffiti. Trains no longer stopped in Lake Shaheen? But why not?

The asphalt parking lot was cracked and riddled with weeds. Still, Texas Hots Café remained, across the road in a partial block of small stores. Nola's Hair, Skin & Nails Salon, Doug's Baits, a laundromat, a vacuum cleaner repair with a CLOSED sign hanging askew in its window. Farther up the road, children were playing and shouting.

I drove slowly, I backed up to peer at the railroad bed. It was elevated to a height of about three feet and so there was an incline, a bumpy incline, at the crossing that would have slowed my mother's speeding car. On the long hill Momma had been frowning in concentration, braking her car, accelerating her car, and again braking, and accelerating; as the panicked cries of her children filled the car—"Momma! Momma! *Mom-ma!*"—and the noise of the train became deafening. For this was not a calculation one could attempt more than once. This was not a calculation that would allow revision.

I thought that must have been it. The realization left me calm and oddly unmoved, like the conclusion to a formal syllogism in logic.

In a symposium last winter at the Institute, the Director had presented a paper with the title "MetaTruth." It was the Director's theory that truth often leaves us unmoved—"We prefer half-truths, meta-truths or outright lies. Because truth allows us no more freedom, and human beings crave freedom."

I think this must be so. I'd had the opportunity to report Zedrick Dewe to the police, I might have brought them the blood-soaked necktie in the envelope he'd left for me, but I had not. And I would not.

•   •   •

Only two vehicles were parked in front of the Texas Hots Café. It was a drowsy time of day, mid-afternoon. The bar area looked closed, but there was activity in the diner-like restaurant. I sat at the counter and ordered a cup of coffee and I went to the public pay phone on a wall at the rear; I looked in the local telephone directory where I found just one *Quade*, and three *Milners*, my mother's maiden name. I dialed one of the *Milner* numbers and after the phone rang four times I hung up quickly, relieved.

Ridiculous, my hands were sweating. I was so frightened, and why?

When I returned to the counter, the middle-aged waitress was smiling at me. I saw her shrewd friendly eyes take in my clothes, my frayed running shoes. Very likely, the scar tissue on my jaw. Women look for rings: she would have seen that I wore no wedding ring. I was alone. I was a stranger. She asked where was I from; if I'd been in Lake Shaheen before? "Yes," I said ambiguously. "A long time ago." In a booth beside the cash register sat an elderly man whom I seemed to know was related to the waitress, or had something to do with the café; he was squinting at a newspaper, idly turning pages with a badly palsied hand. He listened as I told the curious waitress that I was from New Jersey and that I'd been born in the Lake Shaheen area and had been gone since 1971.

"My last name is 'Quade.' My family lived up the Shaheen Pike, about five miles away." With child-like exactitude, I pointed in that direction.

The woman was very quiet suddenly, pouring coffee into my cup. I knew, as I'd known with the fair-skinned man at the gas pump, that the name *Quade* meant something to her, and she wasn't comfortable with the meaning.

No one spoke and so I repeated " 'Quade' "—as if taking a perverse satisfaction in the sound. "My parents were Duncan and Hedy. They both had families here. My brother and I almost died in a car crash, just out there. My mother was driving." *Drinking and driving* I'd almost said. "It happened just out there, where a train was going by." Again I pointed. As if the waitress, staring at me, wouldn't know where the railway crossing was.

She said quietly, "You'll want to talk with my father. Dad?"

Her father was the elderly white-haired man in the booth, who pushed his newspaper aside when I repeated my name, and stared at me with a look of disbelief. "You were the little girl in the car? *You?*"

I told him yes, I supposed I was.

"The little Quade girl . . . !"

I hated his old-man stare, that left me nowhere to hide. I wanted to hide my face, or laugh rudely.

I asked, had he known my parents? "My father was Duncan Quade, my mother was Hedy Quade . . ." I heard myself saying *was,* not *is.* I broke off, confused.

"Hon, sit down. Sit right here. So I can hear you better."

I joined him in the booth. I sat across from him, warming my hands on my coffee cup. Suddenly I felt that everyone in the café was trying to hear us. The woman behind the counter drifted away to wait on another customer, leaving me alone with her father.

He asked my name, and I told him.

" 'Lorraine' it was then."

He asked where I lived now, and I told him.

"But I'm not sure if I will be going back. I don't know."

He asked where my mother Hedy Quade lived now, and I told him in a faltering voice that I wasn't sure. "My mother and I have been out of contact for some years."

"Well, hon. That happens, don't it? In some families."

I wanted to say I didn't know. I didn't know what went on in families. I raised my coffee cup to my lips, and it was a heavy cup, and my hand would have trembled if I hadn't steadied it with my other hand. I was feeling the excitement you feel when, almost without realizing, you've been pressing a car's accelerator down, down. When the car's speed begins to increase and you find yourself thinking how easy, how easy the leap of speed, the rush of concrete, the promise of oblivion.

The elderly white-haired man put out his hand to me, awkwardly. He told me his name, that sounded like Eslner, Ensor. He said he'd known my parents, though not well. "Him, your dad, I knew a little better than I did your mother. He came in the café sometimes. Your mother was such a pretty woman . . ." His voice trailed off. He was a man blundering along a path not seeing where he's headed. "It was . . . what happened out there . . . an accident."

"Was it?"

My question was earnest, sincere. After twenty-two years, how badly I wanted to know!

Mr. Eslner, or Ensor, said quickly, "I didn't see it. Any of it. By the time I ran outside the train was stopping, and the car—well, the car was stopped. I came back inside to call the police and I gave my statement to the police, I'd been at the back of the café. Oh, it was a terrible, terrible thing, but I hadn't seen it." He paused, choosing his words with care. "It was a miracle, people said, nobody was killed."

My mother had often said this, too. Over the years. A miracle that God spared us, God intervened. The car's brakes had failed, Momma would claim. *But God intervened.*

I smiled at the elderly white-haired man who had been speaking so kindly to me. "Our lives are mostly luck, I guess? We want to take responsibility when they go well, but not when they don't go well."

"Well. We're only human, eh?"

The old man tapped my hand in consolation. He smiled, showing discolored teeth. I could smell his breath: a dog's breath. I felt a strange stabbing affection for him, that he would lead me to some vision of the truth; for a fleeting moment I recalled, or almost recalled, my grandfather Milner, Momma's father. Old, old. Ancient the man had seemed to me, and frightening.

"You said—you knew my parents? A little?"

"Oh, I was a lot older than them. I knew your dad the way you know people around here, or used to. Duncan Quade was a tall husky fellow. He worked at the stone quarry, eh?"

"I think so, yes."

"It's shut down now, you know."

"No. I didn't know."

"The quarry workers, they were . . ." Mr. Elsner, or Ensor, shook his head in rueful admiration. ". . . what you'd call characters. Big men. Hard drinkers, some of 'em."

"Was my father a 'hard drinker'?"

"Well. No more than anybody else."

This was a tactful answer. I understood that there was more.

As if reading my thoughts the old man said slowly, "Your dad was good-hearted, I always thought. He'd come in here, shake everybody's hand if he was in the mood, he'd buy his friends drinks, get to talking with strangers like they were old friends. He'd leave a decent—a sizable—tip. He'd ask after anybody who waited on him, how their folks were. There was this war going on in Veetnam, you wouldn't remember, you're too young, but on TV there was footage, and pretty raw stuff you'd see, and Duncan Quade said how evil it was, dropping bombs and napalm on people like that. He'd say he felt damn guilty he wasn't there like some of his high school friends, he hadn't been drafted 'cause of his family. He'd talk like that, real serious. D'you know what he said, once?"

I listened eagerly. I had ceased breathing.

"He said, 'I'm gonna bring my kids up to be good people. In their hearts. It won't matter if they're not rich.' Things like that he'd say, and mean it, too. But then, next time he'd come in he might be different, more moody. And you wouldn't want to pry, or push him. You would not." The old man paused, frowning. He was approaching a more difficult terrain. "Now, what they claimed he did to that woman at Good Hope, some of us found hard to believe. And how the trial turned out—that was a real shock to people here. That was why your poor mother . . . that was why Hedy Quade had her troubles, you see. Why some things happened like they did."

Trial. Had I ever heard there'd been a trial? I could not remember.

Hesitantly I said, "Troubles? What were those?"

"Well, when it happened. That woman over in Good Hope. That they said Duncan Quade hurt."

"Hurt, how?"

"Killed her, they said. 'Second-degree homicide.' "

Seeing the look in my face, Mr. Eslner, or Ensor, was immediately apologetic. "You knew this, honey, didn't you?"

I said, "Yes. I knew something."

I was confused now. Of course I'd known, I'd known something. And yet, I had not known. No one had ever told me. If Ryan knew, Ryan had never told me. *Your father killed a woman. Your father killed.*

I had more to ask, but I was feeling tired suddenly. Wanting to lay my head that felt very heavy down on my arms. But my left arm—I saw with surprise that it was badly sunburnt. When?

The waitress was standing by our booth, speaking to her father with an air of reproach as if he, and not Duncan Quade, was the cause of my exhaustion. She touched my shoulder lightly: "Honey, if you need to use a rest room, there's one through there." I realized then that I was crying. Not crying exactly, but my face was in spasms.

I thanked her, and I went to use the rest room, and when I returned I paid for my coffee, and murmured goodbye, and it may have been that someone called after me—"Hon? You're forgetting your change."

My father was a murderer. My mother fled with us in shame.

Awkwardly I climbed up onto the railroad tracks. Cinders

loosened and slid beneath my feet, I grabbed at tall prickly weeds to get my balance. In the bright May sunshine my eyes smarted. I began walking along the tracks in the direction in which the train had been rushing, that day. In the direction in which the mangled car had been dragged.

I was walking swiftly but awkwardly. Something about the space between the railroad ties made walking difficult. I kept imagining that I could feel the ties vibrating. A train rushing at me from behind. My thoughts were agitated and unsettled. My legs were weak. I was distracted by objects in the corner of my eye. A movement, but it was only a scrap of newspaper blown in the wind. In a culvert beside the tracks I saw broken glass, twisted metal, items of clothing. Like bodies of the fallen. Filth-stiffened children's clothes.

And graffiti in Day-Glo colors: LSHS Class of '92. MICK SUCKS! BIG AL LIVS!

My father, a murderer. My mother, shame.

The most striking visual phenomenon of railroad tracks is how precisely they parallel each other. How, when you stand in the middle of the tracks, shading your eyes, you see how the tracks move inexorably toward the horizon, and become the horizon.

16

---

18 May 1993:
Lake Shaheen, New York

"Tell me what you remember of them, Aunt Agnes. Please."

I wasn't begging exactly. Only just pleading.

"I don't see what good that would do, Lorraine." My aunt Agnes Milner spoke with a frugal twist of her lips. She turned out to be one of those older persons who weigh actions, even words, in terms of *what good that would do.*

"Anything you could tell me, Aunt Agnes . . ."

I wasn't accustomed to making pleas. I wasn't accustomed to such direct, personal emotion. But then I wasn't accustomed to being in the presence of a blood relative, whom I had not seen in twenty-two years.

"Well. We never talk about it here. To her family, your mother is . . ." Agnes paused, frowning. Was she going to say *gone, dead to us?* ". . . a woman who made her decision, to break with us. She will have to live with that now."

"This isn't about my mother, Aunt Agnes. It's just me. My mother doesn't know I'm here."

I could have added *My mother doesn't know I'm anywhere*.

Agnes Milner, my mother's older sister, gazed at me doubt-fully. She was a woman in her late fifties who'd never married; a woman who had spent most of her adult life, as she'd already in-formed me, taking care of her elderly, ailing parents ("Since Hedy was quick to abandon us, early on"); a woman of whom other women would say with pitying shakes of their heads *Oh she's let herself go, poor thing*. Yet you could see that my aunt had been at-tractive, once. In the slack, sullen, fleshy folds of the woman's face you could see a girl's face; a pretty doll-face like Hedy's had once been, or mine.

I had called *Milner, Agnes* just shortly before. And when I'd first stepped out of my car in the driveway of my aunt's house on Rocky Mount Road, just north of Lake Shaheen, my aunt was waiting for me, a woman about five feet five, weighing perhaps 170 pounds, staring at me with teary eyes. We stumbled together and hugged. (Did I remember Aunt Agnes? Not really.) "Lorraine? Little *Lorraine*? My God, it is you." Crushed in this stranger's em-brace I shut my eyes; her flaccid but strong arms, her bulbous breasts pressed against my narrow chest. No one had hugged me with such emotion in a long time: no woman. Yet within forty minutes inside Agnes Milner's tidy little house, the emotional in-tensity began to subside like air leaking from a balloon. I saw my aunt eyeing me with something like suspicion. *You are Hedy's daughter. What do you want from me?* For I must share in my mother's blame for the disappointment of Agnes Milner's life.

Agnes worked in a chiropractor's office in town—reception-ist, bookkeeper. This small house she owned, in a neighborhood of similarly small houses and grounded mobile homes, she spoke proudly of having "purchased, myself, for cash" after selling her parents' house after her father's death in 1986. "I'd tried to get in contact with Hedy, thinking at least she'd want to know that our parents were gone, but there was no way. She'd seen to that."

Agnes sniffed. The old wound was fresh, still bleeding. She was waiting for me to reply, but how could I defend my mother?

"The old house, they left to me. With thirty acres. Their will stipulated 'our loving daughter Agnes.' They left some money to my brother Boyd, not that Boyd needs money. *He's* out for Number One, like Hedy always was. It was the least they could do for me, they said."

I tried not to wince. My aunt, whom I had not seen in twenty-two years, whom I wanted so badly to like, the kind of person who utters with mean satisfaction *The least they could do.*

Unlike my elderly friend at the Texas Hots Café, Agnes Milner wasn't overly concerned with sparing my feelings. Once she began, she took up her subject with zest, a gardener pruning back rosebushes with a sharp shears. *Snip-snip-snip* for the bushes' good. Her complaints about Hedy went back to childhood. "Because she was so pretty, your mother was led to believe that she could always get her own way. Oh, everybody had to love *her*, and loving her they'd forgive her. Then she met Duncan Quade." Agnes spoke grimly. Yet, as she spoke, she was eating; she expected me to eat, too. We were sitting in her kitchen breakfast nook, as she called it, with an immense walnut coffee cake the size of a hub cap before us. "Duncan Quade, he was a good-looking man, and he knew it. Well, he was good at heart, too.

Only just hot-tempered. The jealous type. Him and Hedy, they got married too young." Agnes paused, I waited for her to hint that the wedding had had to be speeded up, but she refrained. Though allowing me to draw my own conclusions. "Duncan was one of them typical stone quarry workers, that need to drink and have a good time, but can turn quarrelsome. He'd give you the shirt off his back, like the saying goes. Once, he pulled my car out of a ditch where I'd slid in, after an ice storm, used chains he carried in the back of his pickup. He'd do things like that for anybody, and never accept payment. But he had a drinking problem, like all of them back then. And Hedy, too. She got it from him I suppose, and she got it bad. She had a jealous streak, too. Duncan began complaining to people his wife gave him so much grief he couldn't live with her which was why he moved out. And he'd move back in, and out again. 'Cause there were other women in your father's life, Lorraine. I'm sorry to be so blunt, but there you are. Before he married your mother, and after. There's plenty of men like that, if you marry one of them you have to accept his nature. Hedy was all hysterical and I told her, look: you knew you were taking Duncan away from some other girl who loved him, didn't you? (Because we both knew this poor broken-up girl. Everybody knew.) And Hedy said, 'But I thought Duncan really loved *me.*' " My aunt laughed at such naiveté. She knew better, of course. "Anyway, Duncan had his women he'd known before Hedy, and he wasn't going to give them up. One of them lived over in Good Hope, and people said she boasted she'd had Duncan Quade's baby, but Duncan always denied it, at least to his family on this side of the lake. Oh, you couldn't believe that man," Agnes said, shaking her head in rueful admiration, "he'd say anything he thought you wanted to hear, and every time you'd want to believe him. Like, at the trial—"

I waited. Hoping my aunt wouldn't realize that I didn't know about the trial.

"—it came out this woman had relations with other men, and the lawyer for Duncan tried to argue that any one of them might've killed her, could be it was a 'drug deal gone bad,' except nobody else was placed there at the scene, the woman was by herself that night. People said she was a hippie slut that got what she deserved but two dozen stab wounds, my goodness!—whoever did it sure hated her. Your father always denied it, went kind of crazy in the courtroom saying he'd never have done it, such a thing. Tried to say how he'd gotten her blood on him, trying to lift her up where he found her, 'cause she was still alive then, but he was the only one placed at the scene, they said. And he'd been drinking, and he was high on—what's it called—'speed.' Oh it was an ugly disgusting time for us. On TV, in all the newspapers, you couldn't hide from it—the name 'Quade.' Hedy, she tried to hide from it, best as she could. That was her way—to hide, and drink. She kept you and your brother home from school. You don't remember, you were just a little girl." Agnes looked at me shrewdly. "Do you remember?"

I allowed her to think yes, I remembered.

"The thing was, Duncan Quade had a reputation for being 'prone to violence.' I wasn't at the trial but people said he made a bad impression on the court, giving testimony, he couldn't keep his temper even then, started shouting at a man questioning him.

The jury was out just a day. 'Second-degree murder.' The judge sentenced him to 'twenty-five years to life.' "

Agnes paused, breathing hard. As she'd begun to speak more rapidly, she'd begun eating more rapidly. I was staring at her face, her prim snail-mouth. Twenty-two years of not-knowing, and now, so much knowledge heaped on me, I felt numbed, battered. "Except: Duncan Quade died in prison. Attica, it was. You have heard of Attica? Some other inmate stabbed him to death, he died on that day your mother got drunk and had her 'accident' with you kids. That day."

"*That* day?"

"The warden's office at the prison called her, that morning. To inform her that Duncan had been killed. They were still married, you know. Hedy had never filed for divorce. In our family, nobody knew that Duncan was dead, we got a call from the Lake Shaheen police saying that Hedy had had an accident, at the railway crossing—"

April 9, 1971. Always I had thought this was the date of my near-death and it was the date of my father Duncan Quade's death.

"I—I hadn't known that, Aunt Agnes. That day . . ."

"Well. We tried to keep it from you and your brother. Such ugly news." Agnes spoke less sternly, as if relenting in her *snip-snip-snip* frontal attack. She wiped at her eyes; for a moment it seemed she might cry, and that I might cry; for crying is contagious, especially at close quarters; then she rallied, with a mouthful of walnut coffee cake. "Oh, Hedy had a breakdown—I guess you'd call it. On TV, you see women interviewed all the time, they 'crack under stress' or it's 'trauma this,' 'trauma that'—some of 'em even kill their own children. After that accident, Hedy wasn't ever right. She'd broke her hip bone, and her pretty face wasn't so pretty any longer, and she was hardly out of the hospital when she began drinking again, and tried to get her hands on all the painkillers she could. You'd think that woman would give thanks to God that she was alive, and her children alive and not crippled, but, well—her mind was affected, I think. She was too ashamed to live in Lake Shaheen any longer, she said. Poor Ryan, you know, should've had more physical therapy, but no, Hedy took him away. She wouldn't listen to any of us! I drove out to her house and she refused to let me in, there I was standing out on the porch pleading with my sister not to drive off in that camper, and Hedy inside not answering me. Oh, I was sick with worry for her! I said, 'Hedy, you're crazy to go away like this! Here is where your family is, here's where people love you.' But she would not listen. Her judgment was impaired. She left without saying goodbye, and took poor Ryan, who was still on crutches, and you—you with your little face not even healed. We heard from her only a few times, telephone calls when she sounded drunk. Saying, 'I see him. He's hunting me. Oh Agnes, he's waiting for me in hell!' And before I could get out of her where she was, she'd hang up. What kind of a life was that, your mother led?"

A desperate life. A broken life.

A guilty life.

I said, smiling stiffly, "It wasn't always that bad, Aunt Agnes. Some times, we were happy enough. Broken lives are still lives."

"Well. You'd say so, I suppose."

"Momma was always an interesting person, a 'personality'—sober or drunk, clear-minded or paranoid. Much more interesting than most mothers, I would guess."

Agnes glanced at me sharply. My sudden tone—detached, analytical—wasn't one with which she was familiar. It went against the grain of her expectations of one of Hedy's scarred children!

"I seem to forget, you are her daughter, Lorraine. You'd have that point of view."

"I'm his daughter, too. I loved them both."

Primly Agnes wiped her mouth of sticky crumbs and pushed the plate from her. She said, nodding so vehemently that her face seemed to be shaking loose, "But there was justice, after all. Duncan Quade wasn't in Attica but three months before another inmate stabbed him about as bad as he'd stabbed that woman. So there was justice, people said."

To this, I had no reply. I was sitting calmly, the palms of my hands pressed against my eyes. I wasn't crying, but I might have given my aunt that impression.

"Well," she said, faltering, "there should be justice, shouldn't there? An eye for an eye . . ."

I allowed my aunt to think, yes this was so.

I asked, "What was the name of the woman who died?"

"The woman who—? *Her?*" Agnes frowned at me, as you'd frown at an impetuous child. "We did all we could to forget that name."

"But do you remember?"

"No."

Agnes spoke so vehemently, I knew she must remember. I waited for a beat or two, in silence.

"Lorraine, why dredge up that old, ugly history? Duncan Quade paid for his sins, let him rest in peace." Agnes paused, picking at the coffee cake with her fingers, and eating. "I think her name was some strange foreign name. 'Deworsoff'— 'Deworsofski'—something like that."

Deworsoff. Deworsofski.

"A hippie slut of a woman," Agnes said bitterly. "If it hadn't been for her . . ."

I thanked my aunt politely for the coffee cake, which I hadn't touched. I thanked her for speaking with me, and said that I had to leave.

Agnes blinked at me in surprise. Why, I'd only just arrived, she protested. There were other relatives who would want to see me—"I'll call them, Lorraine, right now."

I murmured thanks. But I couldn't stay.

I was driving on to Olcott, I told her.

"Olcott? Who do you know in Olcott?"

My aunt sounded hurt, baffled. In retrospect I would see that she had assumed our blood tie to be such, I would surely remain in Lake Shaheen for a while; if I'd returned at all, surely it was to re-establish a connection with the Milners; if she'd been a little harsh with me, surely I would forgive her?

Protesting, Agnes followed me outside to my car. She was breathless, red-faced, accusing. As if, after all, I were an emissary of Hedy's whom she should never have trusted.

As I climbed into my car, Agnes called out sharply, "Where—

where is your mother now?" It was the one question she'd been wanting to ask me since I'd arrived.

I had to tell my aunt, I didn't know.

Wanting to add, in Hedy's querulous voice, that her whereabouts were her own damn business.

17

Christmas 1974:
Albuquerque, New Mexico

You *kids! See what I brought you.*

A Christmas tree. Not a cheap tinsel tree but a real evergreen.

The sudden smell of evergreen needles, in the stale air of the motel room.

Half-price, 'cause it's Christmas Eve. C'mon, help me!

Trimming the tree Momma called it. Like we used to do when I was a little girl. Where there was snow, a long way away in the Chautauqua mountains.

In this place we were now at the edge of the desert there was wind, wind, wind and sun that made your eyes dazzle. But there was no snow.

Why's it *trimming?* Ryan demanded in his whining voice but Momma ignored him, Momma was humming to herself and smiling, holding a cigarette in her left hand. Why d'you call it *trimming?* The tree was as tall as Ryan and had some broken hanging-down branches still it was a beautiful tree, I shut my eyes smelling the evergreen needles. Ryan was getting excited, asking loudly why's it *trimming,* Momma why's it *f-fucking t-trimming?* Ryan did not like words used strangely, or words that sounded strange, or words he did not understand, you could see him struggle to comprehend like trying to swallow something too large for his throat, and when Ryan couldn't comprehend he became excited and anxious and angry. His hands that were bruised and scabby from cuts twitched as if he wanted to hit something, if Ryan walked or ran in such a state his left foot dragged like a weight. Saying, his lips damp with saliva, M-Momma I'm asking, why the f-f-fuck you call it *t-t-trimming?*

Momma ignored him, as if Momma was thinking Ryan would stop if she ignored him, but I was wishing Momma would not 'cause it made my brother more excited when anybody ignored him. F-F-Fucking t-t-t-*trimming,* Ryan said loudly, and I giggled, pressing my hands over my ears for Ryan was saying this bad word you were not supposed to say. At school especially you were not supposed to say. If you were a girl you were not supposed to say. Momma's cigarette dangled from her red-lipstick mouth as she shook out a strip of glittery silver stuff to hang on the tree branches. We are *trimming* the tree, that's what people do and what we are doing, it's Christmas Eve Momma said in a bright happy voice. Saying, Lorraine sweetie, c'mon help me. I was Momma's little helper, Momma said. When Momma loved me best, that was what Momma said. Words like that. Ryan was twelve years old and his scalp was raw and patchy where he'd yanked out hairs. Ryan was skinny and mean as a rat Momma said. Momma was only just teasing saying this, a way of Momma's like tickling. I was nine years old and Momma's sweet little doll-face she could cuddle to death except when I was a pain-in-the-ass-worse-than-your-brother.

Momma teased but Momma did not mean it she insisted.

Momma could say the cruelest things but then laugh and hug you kiss the top of your head saying, Oh sweetie: just kidding!

Momma was in her stocking feet up on the vinyl motel chair and leaning her hand on my shoulder, hard. So I worried I would fall, and Momma would fall and be angry. Momma's face was flushed and almost-pretty from the outdoors, the cold wind and who she'd been with before coming back to us, one of Momma's trucker friends maybe who gave her money and on Christmas Eve he might've given her a lot of money so Momma was in a happy mood except for bratty Ryan, and her face squinting like an old woman's against the cigarette smoke. And Momma cough-cough-coughing. Ryan said sneering, Lookit this shitty tree you brought back, Momma lookit the needles falling. Why'd you bring us such a shitty tree Momma, I'm asking you. At the schools we went to Momma came to explain my son has a certain injury to his *cere-bell-um*, the *cere-bell-um* is part of the brain, motor and speech coordination, but Ryan is a good boy and a smart boy. A little nervous sometimes. High-strung sometimes. Like one of them, what d'you call it, dalmation dogs. Shivery all over like they could jump out of their skin, and you have to watch they don't nip at you. But my son is a good boy at heart.

Ryan was saying, kicking at the tree, This is a sh-sh-shitty tree, I hate this sh-shitty t-tree, you can f-f-fucking t-t-t-*trim* this sh-sh-shitty tree your fuckin' *selfs*.

Still Momma was trying to ignore Ryan. Hanging strips of glitter on the tree, I handed to her. At the drugstore she'd bought a box of six glass ornaments. Shiny red, covered in frost. Plastic icicles.

A Styrofoam Santa Claus with a fat-cheeked red face holding a can of Coors in his right, mittened hand, Momma found in the trash.

You kids c'mon, it's Christmas Eve. No snow, but it's Christmas Eve. Give thanks we're alive, it's Christmas Eve. Momma blinking runny black ink from her eyes saying, You kids are all I have.

I told Momma I loved the tree. I told Momma what I wanted for Christmas was my doll Bessie, I still remembered.

I told Momma I loved the tree, I did not mind that some of the branches were broken and there were brown needles falling off onto the motel carpet, I was not angry at Momma for being gone so long we were watching TV and the picture all blotched and zigzaggy and we were eating stale taco chips and pimento dip and drinking Pepsi from the two-quart plastic container, I told Momma I loved the tree better than anything in the world so Momma would hug me and not Ryan, so Momma would love me best and not love Ryan at all, and Momma stooped to hug me and kiss the top of my head in that way that made me shiver, like I was a baby still and my skull soft. I could feel Momma leaning hard on me, and losing her balance, in her slippery stocking feet on the chair, and on my other side there was Ryan jeering, Shitty

shitty shit-shit-shitty t-t-tree— And out of meanness Ryan kicked at my legs, and Momma lost her balance turning to swat at Ryan, Momma fell onto me, Momma on her knees on the floor crying in fury and pain and Momma pushed me aside to grab Ryan who was laughing Hee-haw, hee-haw, his donkey laugh that was forbidden. Momma shook Ryan by the shoulders and slapped Ryan, afterward Ryan's nose would be bloody which only made him laugh, Momma was sobbing like her heart was broken, Oh you little beast, you're my judgment aren't you, my hell on earth aren't you, why didn't you die like you were meant, fucking little beast.

Oh God I see him everywhere. I know he's gone, but I see him. And he sees me.

Momma was white-faced, terrified. It was Christmas day, she'd been gone again. There came Momma clawing to shut the door, slide the bolt, draw the heavy drapes that smelled of cigarette smoke. There came Momma stumbling in her high-heeled shoes smelling like spilled whiskey. The Days End Motel at the edge of the city. We had been here for a week, or a month. We would leave next morning in the camper, we would leave the dying Christmas tree behind.

Waiting for me in hell, oh God I know.

18

---

19 May 1993:
Olcott, New York

"I want my father's watch back. You have no right."

Next day I drove seventy miles north and west to Olcott, on the south shore of Lake Ontario. The immense lake, an inland sea, began to lift out of the hilly farmland with each mile, like an encroaching dream at the horizon. A hazy blue, a pale gray-blue stretching out flat, for as far as I could see, gradually becoming the horizon. The landscape through which I drove—nearing the lake, it was increasingly farmland, fruit orchards—was one of serenity and beauty and yet my mind was agitated, like something shaken.

I was seeking Zedrick Dewe. I was making a mistake, possibly.

I had no reason to think he might be in this region. Except the box of matches. No reason to think I would ever see him again, to confront him.

"God damn you! Breaking into my . . ."

It was a dangerous thing I was doing. Possibly.

He was a dangerous man. This was a fact.

He'd sent me the Director's bloodied necktie, to taunt me. He had seemed to know that I wouldn't turn it over to the police.

Instead, I'd thrown the necktie away. I'd known what it was and what it meant and I'd thrown it away. In fear, and in loathing.

Yet: *Our deepest motives are opaque to any introspection.*

This had been my belief, since adolescence. Long before I'd acquired a vocabulary with which to express it.

There, on a bluff above the lake, outside the small lakeside town of Olcott, was **Otto's** White Horse Tavern. It was old, made of logs stained a deep russet shade; it looked like a hunter's lodge in the Chautauqua Mountains, except for the flicker of neon signs advertising beer and ale. Tall gnarled trees grew close by, the largest partly split as if it had been struck by lightning; in such proximity to the lake, lightning strikes were frequent. I saw with relief that the sky above the lake was hazy but cloudless, at the moment. It was early evening, sinking toward dusk.

Otto's White Horse Tavern with its scrub-grass front lawn and part-filled asphalt parking lot made me think of my father, Duncan Quade: this tavern was very like the taverns my father had patronized, maybe a little better than most. It excited me to think of Duncan Quade whom I could barely remember (unless I remembered Daddy too well) and now when I remembered him I must also think *My father was a murderer, a murderer was my father.*

Yet stubbornly I thought *I loved him anyway. No one can change that.*

In my ignorance, I'd never given any thought to the daughters and sons of murderers; individuals exposed in the media, caught in the glare of flashbulbs, and nowhere to hide though they are innocent of their parents' crimes. I'd never given any thought to the families broken and humiliated by the actions of criminals though I was a daughter of such a family myself. Thinking now *Momma did the right thing, maybe. To take us away.*

It was an entirely new thought. For always we'd blamed her, Ryan and me, for uprooting our lives, denying us relatives, longtime friends, a hometown. Especially we'd blamed her when we were older, and able to see for ourselves the contrast between our aimless itinerant family life and the normal-seeming lives around us. In Missouri, in Kansas, in New Mexico, in Arizona. Wherever we'd drift to, and stay for a while.

You kids! You are all I have. How Ryan and I hated our mother for saying this, it was such a claim of selfishness. Now I was beginning to see it might simply have been the truth.

I'd left her, at sixteen. Ryan had dropped out into a life of drugs and petty street crime, years before.

Ryan: I was feeling sharply how I needed to see my brother, speak with him again soon. I dreaded to think that Ryan might no longer be alive . . .

Inside the tavern, there were ten or more men crowded at the bar, and not one woman. I was made to feel self-conscious and yet protected, for the bartender was affable, asking, "What c'n I do for you, honey?" as I approached.

Honey. I smiled to think how far I was from Princeton, New Jersey. Both in miles and in time.

I ordered a glass of beer. I tried to drink it: the sharp pungent taste reminded me of my father, and for a moment I was confused about why I was in this place. Not Duncan Quade who'd died in 1971 in Attica, but a man named Zedrick Dewe was my object.

I wondered if the bartender was **Otto**: a man of youthful middle age with long, ripply white hair in the style of a folk-rock musician of another era. Clearly he was a bodybuilder; his neck, shoulders, upper arms and torso were impressive. Yet there was a gallant quality to the man, a kindly paternal air. When one of the men at the bar tried to start a conversation with me, and the bartender saw that I wasn't encouraging it, he came over to position himself in front of me, busily drying glasses. At a strategic moment, when no one would overhear, I asked, "Do you know a man named 'Zedrick Dewe'? He comes in here sometimes."

I didn't know if this was true. Yet I heard myself speak the words with girlish sincerity.

The bartender frowned, and slowly shook his head.

"He's tall, he's about thirty years old, his hair is shaved up the sides and back and it's long in front . . ." *He's a brute. He's treacherous. He has assaulted a man, nearly killed him. He nearly assaulted me.* "Possibly his name is 'Deworsoff,' or 'Deworsofski.' "

The bartender said, with a quizzical smile, "You mean 'Dewsofski'?"

"His first name is 'Zedrick'?"

" 'Zed' is what he calls himself, if it's the guy I think it is.

He's from Strykersville. He comes to Olcott sometimes. 'Zed Dewsofski.' Works for a contractor in Strykersville."

"Did he have a mother who was"—I paused, not knowing how to continue, faltering—"who was—killed? A long time ago?"

"Maybe."

The bartender eyed me suspiciously now. "What d'you want with Dewsofski? He ain't a regular here, can't say I know him."

I wondered if this was so. I hoped the bartender wouldn't put in a call to "Zed Dewsofski" as soon as I left.

I said, "I just want to speak with him. I'm grateful for your information, thanks so much. Is your name—are you—Otto?"

Sucking at his mustache, not so friendly as he'd been a few minutes before, the bartender said, with a shrug, "Honey, there's only one 'Otto' in Olcott. And I sure ain't him."

19

1965–1970:
Lake Shaheen, New York

Those years I lived as his daughter. Before he went away and left us, the three of us remaining in the house on the Shaheen Pike Road. Those years not-knowing who he was, who and what he would become in the eyes of others. Yet remembering how, summer nights, Daddy would call us excitedly to come outside, onto the porch, all of us including Momma in our nightclothes, saying *Hear that? That's black bears, up in the mountains.*

Lonely plaintive cries. You had to hold your breath to hear. If you didn't know those were black bears you'd think it was dogs baying, or coyotes.

Daddy lifted me on his shoulder so I could hear better.

Daddy lifted Ryan on his other shoulder. The two of us, holding our breaths hearing the black bears in the mountains. Daddy saying *It's like music, almost, ain't it?*

20

20 May 1993:
Strykersville, New York

" I want that watch back. It's all I want from you: nothing more."

I told myself this. I seemed to believe this.

In the morning driving, mostly uphill, to Strykersville, about twenty miles south of Lake Ontario. An old, inland city on the Erie Barge Canal. Population 22,000. It appeared to be economically depressed as if under a bell jar, no oxygen, arrested in a long-ago time, the early 1960s perhaps. Along the canal, the cinder towpath looked neglected. There were abandoned freight cars, badly rusted, on sidings, and a number of vacant stores, warehouses, small factories. Dark-skinned children played in the streets of the lower city, shouting in my wake.

My senses quickened. I had tracked my assailant down, had followed him to his lair. I who had been the hunted now felt the curious thrill of the hunter.

Z. *Dewsofski* lived at 833 East Canal Road. In the motel in which I'd stayed the night before, I had looked up his name in the local directory.

In the motel, I'd called a colleague from the Institute, at her home, to ask about the Director, and was told that he was "in stable condition, and improving."

Did the police catch the mugger? I asked.

Not yet. But police were "following leads."

I was passing a strip mall, a Kmart. Like a bit of grit blown into an unprotected eye the thought came to me *Don't go to him unprotected! You must have a weapon to defend yourself.*

I laughed aloud, uneasily. In the privacy of my car I often murmured to myself, argued, even laughed. For much in my life had come to seem absurd to me, preposterous: yet it was my life.

A principle of semiotics: all things are signs, but not all signs are things.

It was absurd, I did not want a weapon. I did not intend to confront Z. *Dewsofski* directly. I would enter his living quarters if I could and I would take back the watch he'd stolen from me but I would not confront him directly, not ever.

I parked and went into the Kmart and examined knives. There was a startling quantity of knives, of diverse sizes. No salesclerks hovered near to observe me, to register suspicion. It was an innocent-seeming purchase: a nine-inch stainless steel steak knife with a rubbery black grip, made in Taiwan. My hand was steady lifting the knife, weighing it. In my apartment the furious drunken man had laid his hands on me, bruised me. *Cocktease. Cunt. Think you're too good for me.*

Yes, I needed the knife. I would need to defend myself.

Z. Dewsofski was the son of a woman who'd been stabbed to death. The son of a woman brutally murdered. *Jonquil* had been his mother's name but he had not told me her surname but still I knew the name now, I had tracked Z. *Dewsofski* to his home.

He'd almost raped me. He had manhandled me.

"Because I'm the daughter of the man who killed his mother. Because he hates me."

So that was the bond between us. Drawing me to him, I'd felt powerless to resist.

"Ma'am? C'n I help you?" a cashier called out to me as I drifted toward the Kmart checkout counters. Half of the counters were closed but I hadn't seemed to notice. The young woman took my money and bagged the wicked-looking nine-inch knife as if it were any Kmart household item, stapled the bag, and in the parking lot in my car I clumsily unstapled it, removed the knife and peeled off the sticky labels and placed the knife in my bag.

Not an illegal concealed weapon, was it? Not a handgun.

I wore a khaki-colored baseball cap, a generic cap with no identification, to hide my hair. To hide my eyes, dark sunglasses that left dents on my nose. To hide my body, shapeless-generic boy clothes.

Seeing me he wouldn't recognize me. Not hundreds of miles from Princeton.

There wasn't much traffic on Canal Road as it led away, east from the Strykersville city limits. The Erie Barge Canal ran beside the

road, a wide murky rather oily-looking strip of seemingly immobile water. There must have been a flow, a current, but you
couldn't determine in which direction it was moving. In this low-
ertown time itself seemed to have ceased. Here were railroad
tracks that looked unused, vacant lots, aging commercial buildings—grain mills, small factories—and weatherworn stucco row-
houses. The address on East Canal turned out to be a gaunt
shingleboard house set back in an overgrown lot that looked as if
it had been a farmhouse decades before, though no farm buildings remained. Next door was the partially filled parking lot of
Empire State Precision Tools. Across the road was a small block
of commercial shops, one of them a neighborhood grocery. I
thought with a stab of satisfaction *He's lonely here.*

I did want to punish him. I wanted revenge for myself, and
for the Director.

He had destroyed my new, fantasy life as the favored assistant
of the Director of the Institute for Semiotics, Aesthetics, and Cultural Research. He had done this on purpose, and must be punished.

Beside an immense oil drum at the rear of the Empire State
Precision Tools lot I parked my car, inconspicuously.

From this position I could see into the overgrown backyard
of 833 East Canal. There were wild-growing forsythia bushes in
bloom, vivid sunburst-yellow, amid a tangle of weeds and briars.
There were wan-looking birch trees and at least one tall elm that
had been badly split and damaged by lightning, like the tree at
Otto's Tavern.

High overhead the sky was splotched with thunderhead

clouds from the lake. It was a breezy-cool spring day, nearing noon. The damp grasses smelled fresh, exuberant. In my disguise I thought *No one knows me here, I am invisible.*

I could not have said if I was very excited, or frightened. My thoughts were agitated as moths throwing themselves against a lightbulb.

Yet the house at 833 East Canal appeared to be empty. There was no vehicle in the driveway except an aged hulk of a car at the rear, with flattened tires. At this time of day the man whom neighbors would know as Zed Dewsofski would be at work. I was reasonably certain he would be at work. If a neighbor saw me and asked what I wanted, I would say innocently that I was looking for—who? A name would fly into my head, a purely in-vented name if necessary. I wasn't worried. *I am frightened to death. I don't want to be here.*

The old shingleboard farmhouse had been painted a glaring gunmetal gray and some of the windows were equipped with shutters, newly repaired and painted. The bartender at Otto's Tavern had said that Zed Dewsofski worked for a contractor. He was a carpenter; he was a house painter, possibly; he didn't own this house, but he'd done repairs on it.

I walked without hesitating into the weedy backyard and to the back door of the house. No hesitating meant: I had business here, I was familiar with these premises, possibly I was one of Zed Dewsofski's women friends. *That kind of guy, you know he has lots of women. Uses women like Kleenex.* This was a house in a neighborhood where doors were often unlocked, sometimes left open, screenless. Children and dogs ran freely outside and in. I was prepared to break a window to get inside but the back door wasn't locked, and opened readily. Again I moved without hesitating. I was carrying my black duffel bag with the knife inside. Quickly I shut the door behind me. I was *in*.

As he'd intruded into my life in Princeton, so I was intruding into his life in Strykersville.

Breaking and entering, I supposed this was. One of the numerous charges on Ryan's juvenile record. Except I had not broken any lock or window. Trespass? Criminal trespass?

With a concealed weapon, a nine-inch steak knife.

Look, I'm only coming to get what's mine. What was stolen from me.

I was in a dingy kitchen, where a smell of grease and scorched food made my nostrils pinch. An old refrigerator, a very old stove with a badly stained top. Underfoot the worn linoleum tile was sticky. A faucet was dripping sullenly into a deep, discolored sink and on a grime-encrusted counter there lay a box of Wheat Chex on its side, nearby a half-empty bottle of Gordon's gin. I felt a tug of pity for the man who lived here. Someone who mostly ate out, didn't prepare his own meals.

Lonely. Lonely as you.

Apparently he lived in only three or four rooms of the gaunt old farmhouse, downstairs. The other rooms were unfurnished, empty or used for storage. I supposed that Zed Dewsofski had an arrangement with the owner of the property: he paid a minimal rent for these minimal quarters. I guessed that his occupancy was meant to be temporary yet had probably stretched into years.

A pervasive smell of stale cigarette smoke, unlaundered clothes, paint, turpentine.

I wasn't thinking clearly, yet I believed that my senses had never been more keenly alert. I seemed to be looking through a telescope. My peripheral vision had disappeared. I was concentrating fiercely on what lay in front of me yet I stumbled into the edges of things, cartons on the floor, a guitar that looked tossed down, with broken strings. There were paperback books scattered underfoot, CDs and cassettes, videotapes with orange discount labels—*Blade Runner, Apocalypse Now, The Vanishing.*

In a farther room, that appeared to be a work studio, there were numerous canvases on end, leaning against walls. Here the smells of paint and turpentine were strong. The bare floorboards were paint-splattered. There was a long cluttered work table.

Canvases? Zed Dewsofski was a painter?

I looked at his canvases, that he'd turned toward the walls. At first the paintings seemed abstract, then I saw that they were meant to be clouds. Some were crudely rendered, others more meticulously shaped. The colors were sky-colors, but muted. Thunderhead clouds of the kind blown inland from Lake Ontario; feathery white clouds frail as thoughts floating against a remote cerulean sky; massed, mountainous cumulus clouds; clouds fluted and curved like waves. *Dream-clouds. A man dreaming while awake.* Several paintings were unfinished, and some of these the painter had ruined with angry smearing swipes of his brush. In a corner lay a canvas that looked as if it had been kicked in.

I shuddered. I remembered how my assailant had gripped

my shoulders, his face contorted with rage. How quickly he'd changed from a man to whom I felt drawn to a man who terrified me.

He'd wanted to hurt me so I'd never forget. Rape, kill. He'd hated me so. Almost, I could hear the jeering voice in this room. *You want this, baby. Don't tell me you don't.*

He hadn't raped me. But he'd violated me, taking my father's watch because he knew how the loss would hurt.

Yet: these paintings. Here was a totally different man. I was so taken by surprise, I didn't know what to think.

"He wants something more. He has hope."

In the clutter on the work table I discovered a book on calligraphy and sheets of paper on which elegant scripted letters had been fashioned in black ink. And there was

*L Quade L Quade
L Quade*

My enemy! This man was my enemy. I'd tracked him to his lair.

His bedroom had in fact the look and smell of a beast's lair. It was a narrow alcove at the rear of the house containing a single, sunken-mattress bed, a single yard-sale chair, a chest of drawers, a lone window with no curtains and a cracked, crooked shade. The smell that pervaded was of slept-in bedclothes, hair oil, perspiration, cigarette smoke.

I smiled. My heart beat so rapidly. I felt like a child entering a forbidden adult zone.

"You bastard. You had no right."

I was furious with him! My enemy.

With a child's logic I went immediately to the chest of drawers. I'd seemed to know that my enemy would hide the watch exactly as I'd hidden it, in the top drawer of the cheap pinewood bureau. And there, amid wadded socks and underwear, it was. My father's watch.

"God, thank you!"

I laughed aloud. I was trembling with gratitude, joy. I could not believe my good luck.

For here, as in a dream, my loss was returned to me: my father's old made-in-Taiwan watch. Here, the stretch band that was gold-plated on the outside and some sort of cheap discolored metal on the inside. The watch's small hands, unprotected by glass, were still at 11:17. Day, night?

I wondered for the first time when my father had died. Had it been day, or night? The telephone call had come to Hedy in the morning, but that didn't mean he'd died at that time; he might have died hours earlier.

I slipped the watch onto my wrist, that was far too thin for it. Immediately I felt a kind of comfort.

I smiled, triumphant. I might have been eight years old and not twenty-eight.

"Leave! Now."

Suddenly I was giddy, as if drunk. Jubilant as a conquering army.

I stepped onto my enemy's bed, this pathetic sunken-mattress bed, a Good Will bed, contemptible. I jumped on the bed with both feet, laughing like a demented child. I kicked at the soiled pillow. I kicked the pillow across the room.

" 'Cocktease. Cunt.' You'd better get out of here. Now."

Yet somehow I lingered. I was brazen, reckless. I went back to the kitchen and took up the bottle of Gordon's gin, I unscrewed the top and took a small swallow. I wasn't a drinker but I knew, or believed that I knew, that gin had no taste—or was that vodka?—and yet this had a distinctive taste, surprisingly sweet, and medicinal. Gordon's Distilled London Dry Gin. I took another swallow, admired the battered old wristwatch loose on my wrist, and laughed. At my enemy I laughed. For Zed—his very name!—seemed pathetic now, defeated.

"Loser."

It was the cruelest thing you could say to a man. Far worse than brute, would-be rapist.

By my own watch I saw that the time was twenty after twelve, I'd been in this dangerous place for nearly a half-hour.

I intended now to leave, to slip out the back door and shut it carefully and make my way, without haste, unobtrusively, to my car parked at the rear of the adjacent lot, but suddenly I realized that I was missing my duffel bag, and had to go look for it, mildly panicked. My bag, my knife! My weapon of defense.

It wasn't in the living room, and it wasn't in the work studio amid the dream-cloud paintings, and at first I didn't see it in the bedroom, then I saw it on the floor where I'd dropped it, amid a tangle of bedclothes.

I'd brought the bottle of gin with me, and took another swallow.

I was remembering how my enemy had invaded my life, and how he'd left his subtle, and not-so-subtle, marks behind. The stink of his urine in the unflushed toilet, the smudge of grease on a kitchen glass.

Yet, now that I had the watch, now that I could leave in triumph, I was feeling less anger at my enemy. For I had to concede: another man would have tossed the watch away. But he'd taken it instead, and he'd kept it in a safe place. I felt a wave of tenderness for one who would keep the watch in a safe place as I'd kept it for so many years. And I'd been moved, too, I had to concede, by the evidence of the canvases. *He is trying. Hopeless, yet trying.* For no one would care about Zed Dewsofski's art. No one would give it more than a bemused glance. If an artist of repute had signed the paintings, they might have been redeemable; as the work of an unknown in Strykersville, New York, they were worthless.

Well, maybe I was jealous, a little. That Zed Dewsofski should have painted those canvases, should have had hope, where no hope was justified; that my enemy should have had faith in his work, at least at one time, while I seemed no longer to have faith in mine—my "work" no more than research for another, and my research ransacked by that other and published under his name.

I drank more gin. I was becoming accustomed to the taste, and the aftertaste. I recalled how Hedy's deflated spirits would rise, a glass or a bottle in her hand. *This calls for a celebration*

Momma would say with a wink. Her wink and a certain down-turn smile of her mouth signaled *Hell no, there is no celebration, there is no call for a celebration, but fuck that, it's time for a drink and more than a drink.*

There was something else that had touched me, aroused me to tenderness, I wasn't thinking very clearly but—the drawer? Socks, underwear? I pulled the drawer open and saw again the paired socks. Frayed white Jockey shorts, much-laundered white T-shirts. Loose change in the drawer, mostly pennies. A man who saved pennies! I was struck by these sights. I had a vision of Zed Dewsofski returning from the coin laundromat with his laundry and dumping it onto his bed, frowning as he sorted it, taking time to find mates for his socks, even to fold, if carelessly, his underwear. Not seeming to realize the futility of his life.

"Why did you hurt me? You had no reason."

I was feeling wistful now. The gin pulsed honey-sweet and warm in my veins. I couldn't have said if I recalled this sight or if I'd imagined it: the stubble-jawed man gazing at me, his voice lowered and urgent with desire *Take me with you?* and I'd been frightened asking where and he'd replied *Wherever you're going.*

Above the chest of drawers was a framed oval mirror. Before, I'd avoided glancing at my reflection. Now, the gin gave me more confidence. In fact I was feeling that I'd exaggerated the danger, for Zed Dewsofski must be at work; wouldn't be home for hours, for it was only midday; I could stay in this place as long as I wished, now that I had crossed his threshold and was a tres-passer; I could explore his life in secret, and he would never know.

In the mirror my face shocked me: not a doll's placid pretty face with a porcelain skin, but a sly animal-face. My mouth looked as if I were trying very hard not to smile broadly, or laugh aloud. Looking at the paintings, I had removed my sunglasses (but where were they? had I set them down somewhere?) and now I saw my eyes stark, moist, nakedly exposed. There was a reckless merriment in those eyes.

I had loved him, or wanted to. My secret of which I was ashamed.

In the bottom drawer of the pinewood bureau I discovered a packet of loose snapshots, and I sat on the edge of the rumpled bed looking eagerly through them. Some of the snapshots were Polaroids, old and faded. Some were stuck together, and when I pulled them apart they tore. Momma had destroyed most of our family snapshots, or lost them in our travels; I envied Zed Dewsofski, that he'd saved these. As in dreams we feel strangely empowered, protected from harm, so there in Zed Dewsofski's bedroom on his very bed, on which I'd been jumping and cavorting like a crazed child only a few minutes before, I sat looking through his snapshots with no sense of danger. I swallowed small mouthfuls of gin, and gripped the bottle tight between my knees. Predominant in the snapshots were pictures of a fleshy, striking woman with beautiful waist-long blond hair, a mane of hair, sometimes worn loose over her shoulders and sometimes plaited in two thick braids that fell across her breasts; this woman had a bold shiny provocative face, luscious crimson lips, small but shrewd eyes that crinkled at the corners with laughter.

"Jonquil."

I stared at her, this woman who laughed at the camera in defiance of what was to come: her death.

For here was the mysterious woman who'd been stabbed to death in Good Hope, in October 1970. The woman for whom my father Duncan Quade had abandoned his family. The woman who had ruined our lives.

Swine Momma had called her. *Worshipper of Satan.*

I saw no evidence of Satan in that face and body. A sensuous woman, I saw. Jocular, good-natured, possibly short-tempered—not a woman a man could easily dominate. Sexually alert, flirtatious and playful; a woman who enjoyed her body, making love and eating and laughing; not a woman easily broken, not a morbidly religious woman; judging from the set of her jawline and her fattish-solid upper arms, a woman who wouldn't back away from a quarrel, or a physical confrontation. In a sunlit snapshot Jonquil stood beautiful and vibrant, in her late twenties perhaps, amid a garden of shabby sunflowers that had grown to a height of six feet, and she was smiling with her tongue poking out mischievously between her lips, heavy breasts snug in a tight-fitting GRATEFUL DEAD T-shirt. At her bare feet, partly out of the camera's eye, was a small shape that might have been a dog but was in fact a toddler, a chubby dark-haired child crawling in the dirt.

Other snapshots showed the blond woman with this child, now older, clearly her son. He was sprawled on her lap, he was straddling her fleshy thighs, he was squirming and sulky, or laughing up at her with a look of childish adoration. He was a husky boy with deep-set eyes and an angular face and I recognized him at once.

"Zedrick."

Zedrick, with Jonquil. He'd loved her, you could see. Yet he'd blamed her, for dying young and leaving him.

There were a half-dozen snapshots at the bottom of the packet, secured by fraying rubber bands. These were of a tall frowning man in his early thirties, attractive, with broad sloping shoulders and muscled arms and dark thick hair that lifted from his forehead like wings. He wore sports clothes, khaki shorts, swim trunks. His torso and arms, exposed, were covered in a pelt of dark moist-looking hair. In most of the snapshots he was deeply tanned. He held a beer can aloft with a sexy sidelong grin. He sat astride a motorcycle; he leaned against a car; he was waving away the camera, with an annoyed expression; he was laughing at the camera, shading his eyes. He wore a red plaid hunter's shirt, and very dirty jeans with holes at the knees, and beside him was a large tree stump, a long-handled ax embedded in the stump, and there was something blurred in the left foreground, a shape that might have been a lone boot, or trash. In the last snapshot this man was squatting, cigarette between his teeth, smiling, the chubby dark-haired boy straddling his knees.

"Daddy."

I knew, I'd recognized Duncan Quade at once. My young father. My father as he'd been long ago. As I must have known him but could barely recall him.

Duncan Quade, young and handsome and careless. So sure of himself, you'd swear that man had all his life before him.

In a trance I stared at this snapshot for a long moment, and at the others in which Duncan Quade appeared. I looked back at the first snapshots I'd seen, and now I saw, or believed that I saw, Duncan Quade in one or two of these as well, with Jonquil and some others, strangers. I had not seen my father since that August evening in 1970 when Daddy had told my brother and me that he loved us but could not live with us and he'd driven away and we'd run after his car on the road until the red taillights disappeared and we staggered with exhaustion, and now it was May 1993 and I was nearly the age he'd been and I knew that he was dead, I would never see him again.

I fumbled to put the snapshots back into the packet, and back into the drawer. No: I would take one, keep the most precious one for myself, I had the right, I chose a Polaroid of Duncan Quade alone, frowning toward the camera as if only grudgingly was he consenting to have his picture taken *I was young and alive once: here is proof* and the rest I shoved back inside the drawer carelessly. I was very tired now. My eyelids drooped. I needed to find—what had I misplaced? My duffel bag, my sunglasses? I could not leave anything behind. I was frantic not to leave anything behind. I groped for my bag, that had my weapon inside. I swallowed another mouthful of gin. My mouth was now burning, my throat was on fire. The straps of the bag were tangled in my feet but I wrenched them free, and put the Polaroid of my lost father inside the bag, but now my head was heavy, it was difficult to hold my heavy head steady on my shoulders. I made a weak attempt to smooth out the bedclothes that I'd rumpled, where I had been jumping up and down in childish glee. I could not remember why I'd done such a thing. I was feeling wistful, repentant. I tried to determine if I'd tracked dirt onto the bed but my eyes were losing their ability to focus. I lay back, flat on the bed with the sunken-in mattress. It was missing a pillow, I lay flat staring at the ceiling. There appeared to be something crawling on the ceiling—a vine? a crack? a stain in the plaster? The corners of the room had begun to tilt. I was overcome by dizziness, a sick sinking sensation. I shut my eyes, and the room no longer tilted. I needed just a moment to recover. To regain my strength. The gin consoled me *You will be all right.*

I wakened to a sound. It must have been later in the afternoon, the swath of sun had shifted on the wall. Through the window the sky was mottled with clouds. Someone, a man, was standing in the doorway six feet away.

Then he was standing over the bed, staring at me.

I lay very still. I could hear his quickened breathing, and I could smell his body.

He leaned over me, frowning. Needing to determine if I was alive, if I was breathing. For my breath was very shallow. My breath was cunning and shallow as it is in dreams when I'm not certain if I am dreaming or awake, if a predator is actual or will dissolve. I was lying in the sunken trough at the center of the disheveled bed, flat on my back as if I'd fallen from a height and was now paralyzed like a laboratory creature whose spinal chord has been severed. My arms were flung over my head and on my right wrist was the oversized man's watch visible and incriminating. The near-empty bottle of Gordon's gin may have fallen amid the bedclothes. My mouth tasted of sand and may have been agape, spittle may have glistened on my chin. I could not see the man's face clearly but I understood his shock, his surprise. I understood his indignation. His anger. He wore work clothes, he'd been sweating. The heat of his skin touched mine. I felt his humid breath. I tried to speak but no sound emerged. I tried to sit up but I could not move. My legs were without strength as if the tendons had been cut. There was a hot hollow roaring sensation in my head, and in my guts.

The man pulled off my baseball cap, and lay the flat of his hand on my oily forehead.

"You—? How'd you find me?"

21

June 1981:
Phoenix, Arizona

I touched my brother's forehead that was burning with fever. I wasn't going to plead with him *Don't die! Don't leave me alone with her*. Afterward I saw that my fingertips were singed, the fiery throbbing sensation stayed with me for days.

In my brain the perfect ovoid formed.

I was sixteen, and *v. mature* for my age.

After my last exam which was solid geometry. For days I'd been bringing clothes and things with me to school, crammed in my locker. Not that Hedy would have noticed. Handed in the exam booklet and ran out of the gym into the hot dry air that hit me like a furnace blast.

I was free.

Back at the Monte Verde Residential Hotel my mother was sleeping off codeine and vodka from the night before and it would not be her daughter Lorraine's responsibility to rouse her after twelve hours. It would not be Lorraine's responsibility to rouse anyone awake—panicked, flailing, kicking at her—ever again. It would not be Lorraine's responsibility to listen to accusations like a parrot's shrieking. *You always loved him best. Should've sent you to live with him and his whore. You and your junkie brother.*

The plan was a perfect ovoid. The plan was simplicity and no risk.

Other girls at my high school who disappeared, runaways and MISSING, risked their lives with guys. Not Lorraine Quade. Not ever Lorraine Quade who at sixteen (as at fifteen, fourteen, possibly even thirteen) was observed to be *v. mature* by teachers, guidance counsellors, and numerous other Adults of Authority.

Left a note for Momma, of course. Neatly typewritten. Signed with my full name. And no forwarding address, or telephone number.

The plan was I would live with Mandy from the 7-Eleven where I worked after school Thursdays through Sundays. Mandy was twenty-nine, just divorced from her speed freak/drug dealer husband and we got along really well because Mandy was lonely the way I was lonely, for someone for whom we felt no responsibility or guilt.

Mandy and I played gin rummy till 2 A.M., watched late-night TV, listened to country-and-western, bluegrass, soft swingy rock, and Janis Joplin. We brought home frozen pizzas, six-packs of Diet Pepsi, caramel popcorn in giant cellophane bags, tacos so laced with salt the granules clung to our fingers like radioactivity. Mandy and I knew each other's surname but little else about each other. I never spoke to her of Momma except to say *I left and I'm not going back.* Mandy never spoke to me of her ex-husband except to say he was incarcerated at Kingman Maximum Security and wouldn't be giving her or any other woman trouble for a long, long time.

Over Phoenix by night the polluted air glowed phosphorescent.

I would leave, and I would not look back.

The perfect ovoid in my brain. From any angle of perspective, its surface was flawless.

I would learn that my grade for the exam in solid geometry was 98. I would learn that my junior-year average at Phoenix High South was 94. I would work, work, work through my senior year. Craving work the way my brother Ryan craved speed, and finally heroin. *V. mature* and *v. intelligent* was the label. *V. willing to work* was another. I would be awarded a scholarship to the University of Arizona at Tucson and this I would parlay, after three semesters of a perfect grade-point average, into a scholarship to Berkeley where after graduation summa cum laude I would be awarded a fellowship to the University of Pennsylvania where I would earn a master's degree in philosophy in 1988. Like a clockwork doll I had plotted a career course that was free of whim and sentiment as I was free of whim and sentiment.

Last glimpse of Hedy, a puffy-faced woman nodding off to sleep, a glisten of saliva on her lips.

•   •   •

By bus I went to the Phoenix Men's House of Detention where my brother Ryan Quade was incarcerated for auto theft, burglary, breaking and entering. For possession of a "controlled substance," in his case heroin.

Ryan was in the infirmary, in fact. A bored-looking medic told me he had hepatitis-C from an infected needle probably plus heroin withdrawal/anemia/malnutrition from his junkie street-life.

I'd been prepared, I had thought. But you never are prepared. "Ryan? My God."

So weak he couldn't lift his head from the sweat-soaked pillow. His skin was stretched tight as a drum over his jutting bones and skull and was of the sickly yellow hue of rancid chicken. His sunken eyes glowed in his skull like the eyes of a Hallowe'en death's head and several of his upper front teeth were missing. Must've weighed 110 pounds stretched on his five-foot-ten frame. Nineteen and you would not predict he would live to be twenty.

Years before when Ryan was expelled from high school for drugs and had gotten sick, I asked him why, why hurt yourself like this, and he'd told me the drug high was the only time he felt normal or what he guessed was normal. *Don't feel sorry for me, bitch. Sorrow ain't a word in my vocabulary.*

This seemed to be so.

In the infirmary that stank frankly of men's bodies I dared to touch my brother's burning forehead. His eyelids flickered, a look of sullen resentment came over his face. His parched lips moved and I heard, or thought I heard, something like *Fuck off*. I was

fascinated and appalled by the skinny body that, not so long before, had so bullied me; the way an IV tube dripped languidly
into a bone-white ankle. Nineteen and Ryan had been good-
looking once in the sulky-wiseass way of a teen pop star, now he
looked like, as he'd have said in his own vocabulary, shit.

I sat with him. I was allowed forty minutes.

Like papers rustling, Ryan's hoarse voice.

Telling me, ". . . can't leave her, Lor. She needs you."

I didn't inform my brother I'd already left our mother, as I
was leaving him. Didn't tell him with a triumphant smirk *I'm
gone*.

22

———

20 May 1993:
Strykersville, New York

The sunlight faded from the walls of Zedrick Dewsofski's bedroom, and from the window. The sky was riddled with small fierce wind-driven clouds. In the late evening we left the house ravenous with hunger. The air was strangely moist. The tall grasses in the backyard were wet.

It must have been raining, those hours. For now the rain had ceased.

All that matters is, we know each other now.
Know who our father was. That we loved him.

"There's this place on the canal outside town. People know me but won't bother me."

In Zedrick's low-slung rust-speckled Cutlass before turning the key in the ignition he reached over for me in the passenger's seat and framed my face in his big hands another time, and kissed me.

My mouth that was raw from being kissed.

"Lara. I'm crazy about you."

Now it was night, fully dark. Near 10 P.M. we were driving along the Canal Road into the countryside.

We were quiet now, subdued. We had been talking for hours.

We had touched each other during those hours in Zedrick Dewsofski's bedroom, and a little more than that.

In the most technical sense we had not made love. Yet, you could say we'd become lovers.

You want it, baby. As much as I do.

Else why'd you come here? Why'd you stay?

In a trance of discovery, elation. In a trance of disbelief, that happiness could come so swiftly.

Weakly I'd protested, "Zedrick, we can't. We can't do this if we're—"

I couldn't say *brother, sister*. It was a fact too new and too pro-found to be uttered.

Zedrick said, "*Half*-sister, *half*-brother. And we don't know each other, Lara, and we're sure not going to have kids."

Driving now along the Canal Road away from Strykersville, in the night that smelled of rain, wet leaves, the brackish odor of the old canal. In my state of amazement and agitation I noted how natural it seemed, to be beside this man; a stranger, who was also my half-brother; a stranger, about whom I'd been thinking obsessively for weeks.

He'd awakened me from my gin-sodden stupor. He had not

taken advantage of my helplessness. He'd shaken me, gently. He'd pressed a washcloth soaked in cold water against my burning face.

He'd held my shoulders, from behind, as I'd vomited into his toilet.

He had not taken the loose-fitting old watch away from me.

Zedrick Dewsofski was not a man who spoke much, or with ease. You could see that he distrusted words. A man who used his hands, a man who trusted his hands. A man who made his living with his hands and not with words like the men of my acquaintance. Yet, with me, Zedrick was apt to speak eagerly, like one thinking aloud.

"I wai .o see Ryan, too. Just maybe to meet him once. See what the hell there's between us."

"You aren't much alike, you and Ryan. No."

"There's ways people are alike that don't come out till you know them, or they know you. Like, they need to trust you. It would be that way, with brothers."

Brothers. That word.

Zedrick spoke with an air of belligerence, defiance. He wasn't accustomed to being contradicted. At least, by a woman.

You could learn to defer to such a man, unconsciously. At first, it might be pleasurable.

I'd begun to shiver. The rain had chilled the air. And my hair was damp, still. I'd washed it and combed out the straggly kinks and bits of vomit that had splashed up onto me.

Disgusting, I had been. Repulsive.

Yet Zedrick had not seemed to notice for in his eyes I was beautiful.

Had he seen the scars on my face, had he touched, caressed, stroked the scars on my body, had he kissed these, yes and he had said nothing.

I told him that I wasn't sure if Ryan was alive. I was ashamed to admit this.

"Yeah, he's alive. What I heard."

"You *heard*? From who?"

Zedrick, a man of many surprises. He glanced at me sidelong liking it that he had things to tell me about my own family I did not know.

"My uncle over in Shaheen."

"You're in contact with the Quades?"

"Like, I asked them about you, 'Lorraine,' and they said they'd heard you were at some place in New Jersey—'Priceton,' they called it." Zedrick laughed. He was enormously pleased with himself for having tracked me down. "This uncle of mine, what you'd call a great uncle, I guess, 'cause he was Duncan Quade's uncle, said he'd heard that Ryan was in a 'halfway' house in Las Vegas."

Las Vegas? It seemed unlikely, though I wanted to believe.

"Which uncle is this? I stopped for gas at Quade's Auto Repair in Lake Shaheen, and the man who waited on me—"

"Art. Kind of a fattish guy, mid-forties? Freckles?"

"Yes. He wasn't very friendly."

"Did you tell him who you were?"

"Yes. I told him. Duncan Quade's daughter . . ."

"Your side of the family, your mother, see, they think you're their enemies. The Milners."

"But if that man was a relative who hadn't seen me in twenty-two years . . ."

Zedrick laughed. Since that moment of discovery in his house, in his bedroom, on his sunken-in bed, Zedrick Dewsofski had been in an elated mood. His skin glowed ruddy, he exuded a febrile, sexual radiance. I could not keep my eyes from him. I wanted to touch him, stroke his forearm. At the same time I was wary of him, and knew that I must not provoke him.

"See, honey, the Quades and the Milners, in that small town, they hate one another. After our father got in trouble like he did, and what happened to him in Attica, some of the Quades moved away. I don't even know where. The only Quades who I could talk with, who'd listen to me, and believe me, it's just Art and another younger guy who'd be a cousin of mine. They like me O.K. It's not that we see one another much. I drive over, we go out drinking sometimes. I did some painting for Art, that stucco garage you saw, last summer."

House painting, Zedrick meant. It was one of his trades.

He worked for a local contractor, part-time; there wasn't steady employment for carpenters in the Chautauquas. The Niagara region had been economically depressed for years. Zedrick had told me he did carpentry work, house painting, roofing, handyman jobs. Much of it was seasonal, and unpredictable.

Of his painting, his canvases, he'd said with a shrug—"Just things I tried. None of it's finished." I wanted to tell him how striking some of the paintings were, how beautiful and original they seemed to me, but I knew he would react defensively and change the subject. Zedrick wanted to be intimate with me in the ways he wanted to be intimate with me, solely.

He'd wanted to make love. To have sex. That was the swift and easy exchange between a man and a woman. Still, after sex, Zedrick wouldn't have opened himself fully to me any more than I would have opened myself fully to him.

Not yet.

Maybe not ever.

Zedrick was saying, "Where we lived in Good Hope, people were always coming and going. Nobody ever talked of Duncan Quade having some other family, or if they did, I was just a small kid, I didn't know. Duncan was known to be my daddy, but he wasn't always around, and Jonquil wasn't exactly lonely. If Jonquil knew about your mother she'd just have laughed. I was only nine when she died but I can remember her saying, 'Family life is a hoax. It's all bullshit.' I loved Jonquil but even then I wondered if her brain wasn't fried. By the time I was five, six years old I swear I was sharper than her, like adding up numbers, tuning in the TV. She'd fuck up turning on a faucet, practically." Zedrick laughed, in fond derision. Already I had noticed that he never spoke of his mother without laughing in some way that wasn't mirthful.

I thought of Hedy. Hedy living in Lake Shaheen. I wondered when my mother first became aware of Jonquil, living across the lake in Good Hope.

I meant to visit a library in a larger city in upstate New York, to look up information on that long-ago murder case. Duncan Quade, a woman named Jonquil Dewsofski. It must have been lurid, ugly. A "hippie-commune" stabbing. The local media must have loved it: free love, free sex, drugs, a man killing what the papers would call his common-law wife.

The shame of it: Duncan Quade's son in Good Hope had been a year older than his son in Lake Shaheen. For Zedrick was thirty-two, and my brother Ryan was thirty-one. This meant that my father had been sexually involved with the woman who called herself "Jonquil"—and no last name—before he'd married Hedy Milner, as well as after.

After Daddy had left us, Momma wanted us to believe that she'd asked him to leave and that was why he was angry with us, threatened us, "hunted" us. None of that was true, evidently. He had not been stalking us, he'd ceased caring about us.

Anyway, he'd ceased wanting to be Daddy to us.

Love you honey, you and your brother. Just can't live with you right now. Now that I was twenty-eight I thought I understood: my father had been a sexually adventurous man, still young and in good health, and good-looking. He'd married young in the early 1960s and by the 1970s the United States was unraveling, exploding. Hippies, drugs, sex and ear-splitting rock music. Hating the war in Vietnam meant you hated Amerika. Remaining faithful to one individual for life—"monogamy"—was fast becoming a custom as quaintly outmoded as yoking oxen to plow fields.

Jonquil with no last name and no wish to marry, nor even to make a claim on any man, must have seemed to him not only gorgeous and sexy but wise in the turned-on ways of Illumination.

"I don't think that my mother ever knew about you," I told Zedrick. "She never spoke of my father having another child, or alluded to . . . anything."

Cast his lot with swine and with Satan. Poor Hedy, humiliated. A pretty popular small-town girl rejected by her husband for a fattish hippie living in a commune in Good Hope, less than thirty miles from Lake Shaheen. (In fact, Good Hope was less than twenty miles from Lake Shaheen, as the crow flies. But you had to drive around the southern tip of the lake, then north and east to Good Hope on back-country roads.) Speaking of Satan had been my mother's desperate way of trying to cast a moral judgment upon my father's actions. You couldn't blame her, wanting to stir sympathy in others and, in my runaway father, shame.

It had to fail. Maybe he'd loved her, but he couldn't live with her. It would turn out that he couldn't live with Jonquil either, but Duncan Quade couldn't have known that at the time.

I wanted to ask Zedrick *Why do you think he killed her?*

But I knew, I had better not. Not quite yet.

Now I remembered, he'd told me, in my apartment in Princeton, that Jonquil had sent him away at the time. And he'd said something very strange: that, if he'd been with her, he would have been killed with her.

What this meant, I couldn't guess. Not that our father would have killed him, too?

Zedrick was saying, as he drove along the Canal Road, nervously stroking his hair, "Those days! Who somebody's kid was didn't seem to matter. Jonquil went off traveling and left me behind like you'd board a dog with friends, and it was O.K. Once, she was gone for a month. She'd been in Tampa with some guy. She had these stormy relationships, you'd call them, with men. Including our father." Almost shyly Zedrick murmured the awkward phrase *our father*. It was not a phrase you heard in ordinary discourse; it had a religious tone; siblings who spoke of their father would say *Dad, Daddy*. But Zedrick and I had shared no *Daddy* in our childhood. Zedrick said: "I was taught to call all the grown-ups by their first names. Nobody had last names, even. I was taught to call our father 'Duncan' and my mother 'Jonquil'—not ever 'Mommy.' In the foster homes I'd fuck up not knowing what to call anybody. So I didn't call them anything."

I said, "If Ryan and I had called any adult by a first name, we'd have been slapped. It's hard for me to say 'Hedy'—'Duncan'—even now. The difference between Lake Shaheen and Good Hope."

Zedrick said, "One of the differences, honey."

Honey. Not just the word but the casualness of it, the way Zedrick spoke, went through me like a knife blade.

Like sex. Like what he'd done to me on his bed.

I remembered how, taking the snapshots out of the packet from Zedrick's drawer, I had thought *This is it: evidence*. And seeing my young father, my father holding a child in his arms, and that child Zedrick Dewsofski, I'd known. It all came together in that instant. I'd hardly felt a stab of jealousy, the wound had gone so deep.

Daddy. With another child.

I understood now why Zedrick had arranged our meeting in Princeton. He'd sent *L Quade* the ticket anonymously because he was yearning to meet, not me, but his half-sister Lorraine.

Looks like a wedding invitation, Lara, the Institute secretary had said with a smile.

Immediately I had been drawn to him, too. My half-brother. Drinking, and becoming careless. As I never was. That danger zone in which you make mistakes that are in fact not mistakes but your deepest desire. *You want it, baby. Just like me.*

Ask pretty-doll Tina why's a doll fearful of being roughly handled, even in love?

The next several hours passed in a blur. At the Canal House, and after. Like downhill skiers on a slope, Zedrick and me. Descending at the same swift ever-accelerating speed and not knowing where we'd end up.

We ate hungrily, and talked. I was faint with hunger. Zedrick was drinking beer, and I was drinking club soda, still under the heavy spell of the gin and prone to sudden inexplicable tears that Zedrick would wipe away with his calloused fingertips. "Lara, hey: don't be sad. We found each other, didn't we?"

I wasn't sure what he meant by that. What I wanted him to mean.

My brother, my lover. Which?

And, later: "I won't try to force you into anything, honey. I'm not like that. Just, I'm crazy about you. I've never met anyone like you. But I can deal with it."

I wanted to believe this. I thought *He could have forced me, on his bed. That might have happened.*

The risk I'd taken, entering a stranger's house as I had. I would wonder afterward if I'd been deranged.

Deranged, or desperate.

Desperate, or driven.

I might have been raped, strangled. I might have been beaten into a coma by this man's fists, like the Director.

Zedrick was saying in his low urgent voice, "It's enough we know each other, now. Know who the other is. That's all I wanted, see? Almost all."

"And you want to meet Ryan, too."

"Someday. Take me with you?"

I was still wearing my father's broken watch. Seeing it on my wrist, Zedrick had laughed. "So you found it. Sweetheart, you're really something." He seemed to admire me for having tracked him to Strykersville, and entered his house as a thief.

At the Canal House, Zedrick did most of the talking, and ate most of the food. He had a voracious thirst for beer. He exuded an air of hot, erotic energy. I touched his hands, his battered knuckles. You could see he was a man who used his hands roughly. His left thumbnail was blackened with blood beneath the nail. There were nicks and scabs all over his hands. Beside his thick fingers, my own looked slender, delicate. I dared to stroke his forearm that was covered in dark wavy hairs like Duncan Quade's had been, and was sinewy with muscle.

Men who work with their hands. I felt such sympathy for them, and such guilt.

Zedrick was saying, "I don't mean to hurt people, I think I'm a good man at heart. You need to have faith in me."

Why was he saying this? I hadn't been listening, gazing so avidly at his face.

At the house I had wanted to ask Zedrick about the Director.

I could understand why he'd wanted to meet me—why he'd taken our father's watch from my apartment—but why had he assaulted an innocent man, and had he meant to injure him so severely? And why had he implicated me, giving me the Director's bloodstained tie? But the words stuck in my throat. For any words I uttered would be an accusation, a reproach. And suddenly I could not take a side against this man; this man who was my brother; this man who felt so powerful a connection with me.

In any case, I'd become complicit with the assault: I hadn't reported what I knew to the Princeton police.

How can I betray Zedrick, he trusts me.

He has forced me to choose between him and the Director and I have chosen him.

When we entered the roadhouse, which was about seven miles east of Strykersville, Zedrick had walked with his arm loosely draped around my shoulders. It was as he'd predicted: numerous men at the bar called out to him—"Dewsofski! How's it going?"—"Zed! Lookin' good"—but let him alone. They were curious about me, and stared.

I felt the erotic charge, entering the smoky barroom of the Canal House with Zedrick Dewsofski. I felt the men's eyes, assessing. For, seeing us together, you would think we were lovers. You would have to know that we were new with each other, and uncertain of each other.

You would not think, probably, that we were related: half-sister and -brother.

Dewsofski with a woman. Who's she?

Dewsofski with another woman, looks like a stranger.

I wasn't wearing the baseball cap any longer. I'd showered and shampooed my hair and now my hair was curly and fluffed out about my face. Tenderly I'd washed my raw, reddened face. I'd put on makeup. I'd applied lipstick to my mouth that was swollen from kissing. The ways in which Zedrick had touched me with his hands and his mouth had left me breathless and dreamy with that erotic entranced look of a woman who has been loved, and the men in the Canal House saw this, as they might have seen in their friend's face a similar look, of sexual entrancement, at once tender and anxious. And proprietary.

Zedrick steered me to a dimly lighted booth at the rear of the barroom. He'd liked the men seeing me with him, but he wanted me for himself now.

He marveled how I'd found him, and what it meant that I'd waited for him to come home. "See, you wanted me. I'd been thinking you might be my enemy, I mean you'd think that I was your enemy. But—"

Zedrick smiled in that way that reminded me, I realized now, of my long-ago father. A smile that slyly pleads *No need to judge me, honey just love me.*

Zedrick agreed, he'd made "some mistakes." He wasn't exactly sorry, he wanted me to know.

I thought he might be alluding to the Director. The "mugging." I could not ask him, so bluntly. I had no wish to offend this man who reminded me of all that I had lost.

Zedrick went on to say, "Lara, see, I had the feeling, in Princeton, that you knew who I was. Right away, when we saw each other. There's my girl, I thought. I'd always thought that you knew about what had happened when my mother was stabbed to death, and our father was blamed for the murder, and what happened to him in Attica. For sure I thought you'd know my mother's name 'Jonquil' and, maybe, that Duncan had another son. How could you not know? Everybody knew. So I thought you were pretending not to know, like you were too good for me. For us. The bond between us."

Zedrick was breathing quickly, recounting these things. I saw that he was still angry. He would not easily forgive me, for snubbing him. He'd been insulted by my behavior in my apartment, he'd had to think that I was refusing him entry into our common past.

Was it so? Had I lied to my half-brother, denying him?

So much of my doll-life had been lies, partial lies, subterfuge.

I'd learned from both my parents. How shaping words with your mouth can be a way of hiding, not sharing. As I'd hidden Daddy's broken watch from Momma, knowing she'd be furious with me if she found it, and would smash it into pieces in front of me. As I'd searched for Bessie, for days, while Momma looked on smirking and scolding, knowing that I dared not hint to her what was obvious: that my mother was the thief who'd taken my "lost" doll.

And so much of my life as a girl, and as a woman. After I'd fled my mother. I'd fled, I had thought, my tawdry past.

Playing academic games. Games-with-words. Presenting myself to the Director, the most repulsive of human beings, as his ideal doll-protégée.

"Zedrick, I think you're right. I must have known. Not exactly consciously, but . . . 'The bond between us.' "

Zedrick. I loved the name in my mouth, its tawdry small-town glamor.

Zedrick smiled happily. Reached over to squeeze my hand, hard.

"That's so beautiful, Lara. Thank you."

I was falling in love, I believed I knew the symptoms. A sense of weightlessness, abandon. That sensation of floating! And of knowing that you are protected! Like *self-medicating,* a sudden manic gaiety. There is no other person in the world except Zedrick my half-brother, who knows me as no other else knows me. He will protect me. I am an accident victim who has survived the terrible impact of the crash yet is trapped inside the twisted metal and glass hanging in shattered curtains, screaming *Help help me don't let me die*: there is only one way out, one pair of arms to lift you to safety.

He's dangerous. A killer.

I smiled to think it had been said of Duncan Quade long ago that he, too, had been a killer, and in my heart I'd never believed it.

We would leave the Canal House at 1 A.M. Closing time.

I had not been drinking. I was wary of drinking. Falling in love is like losing your footing in a steep treacherous climb. Though I'd had a few sips of beer from Zedrick's glass (I could not refuse when he offered me, could I?) and was feeling child-like, certain that whatever I did was right, I would not be judged.

We'd fallen into the mode of lovers who've acquired a brief—

but very dramatic!—history. In this beery smoky place livened by men's happy drunken laughter, TV tuned to ESPN (a boxing match, twin bloodied faces, black, Hispanic, trapped in an anguish of a struggle as onlookers cheered) and country-rock music blaring from the jukebox. It was bluegrass, that frantic beat. Zedrick leaned his elbows on the table telling me how he'd come home that evening and he'd known right away that someone else was inside: he'd thought it might be one of the neighborhood kids, passed out on his bed from drinking his gin.

"Jesus, honey, what a surprise seeing *you.* I have to admit, I was fucked."

I was fucked. A curious expression. What would the Director make of this linguistic conundrum. To *be fucked* isn't a good thing, is it?

To be taken by surprise. Outwitted, overcome.

Unmanned.

I told Zedrick how I'd taken the box of matches from the pocket of his leather jacket: how it was this that had led me to Olcott, to Strykersville, and to the Canal Road.

I was conscious of enthralling the man with my story. Like Tina, yet capable of speech.

Prettily I said, " 'Otto's White Horse Tavern.' Whoever Otto is, he brought us together, didn't he?"

Zedrick laughed. He drained his glass of beer.

I asked Zedrick how he'd tracked me down in Princeton and he told me it was an accidental thing, he'd heard from some people who knew we were related that I had some kind of "fellowship" in this place they called "Pricetown" in New Jersey.

Zedrick's source had seemed to think vaguely that I was associated with a church, since "fellowship" in this region has to do with Christian church affairs, but he'd figured it out, it had not been difficult to locate me once he knew the place.

"This country is what you'd call 'infinite'—almost. But any town you come to, it's 'finite.' "

I felt a wave of tenderness for the man, that he would say such a thing. As I'd felt seeing his paintings.

So we talked, exchanging tales. The giddy tales of lovers. And even as we spoke, occasionally raising our voices to be heard over the tavern din, I understood that this was probably a mistake, I was probably making a mistake, yet how could I stop myself, I was so happy.

Veering out of control. There's a strange happiness to it, in the reckless instant you surrender.

We were becoming edgy, excited. As we'd been at Zedrick's, in his bedroom. I had not wanted to make love with him but with his hands and his mouth he'd made a kind of love, and I had not stopped him, finally. I had wanted to stop him, but I had not. I'd wanted him so, I wasn't able to push away from him, or resist. Zedrick had known how to bring me to climax slowly and gently, though not so gently at the end; I'd gripped his damp hair in my fingers, bit my lip to keep from screaming, and sobbed as if my heart were broken. *I don't want this. I don't want to love any man.* And taking Zedrick then in my trembling fingers, and he'd ejaculated with a moan into my hands, his face contorted in a kind of pain. And I lay amid the smelly sheets in a daze thinking *This can't be happening, I can't be the person doing such things.* I feared love, I'd seen its consequences. I feared the weakness in love, the madness. The fierce driving need.

In the shower in Zedrick's cramped bathroom I'd washed the smell of him off me knowing that it would quickly return.

Driving to the Canal House, Zedrick pulled me over to sit close beside him in the front seat of the Cutlass. Somberly he said, "Honey, that was just that once. I won't force it. Only, I'm so crazy about you. And I guess—you like me, some?"

23

___

February 1978:
Sun City, Arizona

Momma warned *Don't touch a man unless you're serious. Any man you touch, he's going to touch you back. And the way he does it might not be what you want. It's going to be what he wants.*

Lying on Momma's bed with the heating pad on my abdomen, drowsy from Momma's painkiller she'd given to me with a cup of hot lemon tea like I was someone special at last, and this was something special, staying home from school with my first cramps. Momma was in a teary-tender mood, Momma was stroking my damp headachy head and brushing my hair from my feverish face saying *It's for your own good, honey. To know such things.*

I resented Momma's warning, I was too young: just thirteen.

In secret thinking *I never want to know anything you tell me. I'm not going to be you.*

24

21 May 1993:
Strykersville, New York

The plan was that I would spend what remained of the night in a Best Western Inn about two miles from Zedrick's house, because I was exhausted and needed to be alone and did not want to spend the night in Zedrick's house, and we would meet again next evening at about 6 P.M. when Zedrick came home from work, but when he drove me back to his house, and to my car, he pleaded with me to come inside, he had something crucial to tell me he hadn't wanted to tell me at the Canal House—"It will only take five minutes, Lara. I promise." He spoke so sincerely, I could not doubt him; to doubt him would be to strain the bond between us, which would deeply wound him, I knew. Seeing the expression on my face Zedrick backed off from me, lifting his hands in a playful gesture, saying, "I won't touch you, honey, if you don't want me to, I swear, see?" He was laughing at himself and at me, as I stood irresolute in the driveway, turning the watch on my wrist, and clear and unmistakable the warning came to me in Momma's voice *No: don't. You'll be sorry.*

Yet somehow I must have said yes. Somehow, together with Zedrick Dewsofski I re-entered the house which, more than twelve hours before, I had entered alone and uninvited.

"Then I'll drive you to the Best Western, Lara. You can follow me in your car so you don't get lost."

Zedrick was speaking earnestly, I could see.

I had left my duffel bag inside, in any case.

Zedrick said, in a calm, flat voice, as if this weren't speculation but fact: "Duncan Quade did not kill my mother. Somebody else killed her that night, and he was blamed."

"But—who was it?"

"Could've been anybody. This place we lived in, out in the country, people coming and going all the time, who knows? My father walked in on Jonquil dying, and was the one who got blamed."

In his bitterness Zedrick had forgotten to say *our father.*

I wondered at the calmness with which he'd said *Jonquil dying.*

It had to have been practiced, over the years.

Zedrick had taken a beer from the refrigerator, opened it and was drinking as he followed me into the bedroom, where my duffel bag lay on the floor, kicked into a corner. He was trying to speak in a level voice but I knew he was becoming agitated.

I wanted to console him *I know! I know our father is innocent.* But the words, hopeful as bubbles blown into the air by a child, stuck in my throat.

How futile it seemed to me, two adult children of a long-dead man convicted of second-degree murder, lamenting the past.

"Even if that's true, Zedrick, what difference would it make? We couldn't prove it, and Duncan is dead."

Zedrick said sharply, " 'Cause I want the fucker who killed her to be punished, for Christ's sake. Jonquil was my mother, O.K.? Whoever killed her, stuck her like a dog, I'd like to sink a knife in a few times, myself. Like, in the miserable bastard's gut."

I'd said the wrong thing. I'd said a stupid thing. My face smarted as if I'd been slapped.

I busied myself straightening the bed. Zedrick's bed! Before we'd left for the Canal House, I had remade the bed, but quickly and distractedly. In that dreamy erotic state after orgasm. Now I saw my handiwork more soberly.

Zedrick began to speak less coherently. His face was oily with perspiration. He said he'd been too young at the time to know what was going on. He'd been just a kid, and a fucked-up kid, his mother and her hippie friends had let him puff on their joints, and drop acid at least once—"Not a full dose, just a pin-prick Jonquil said. That was enough." As I made my way around the bed tucking in corners, Zedrick followed me unconsciously, the way a child might follow his mother, not wanting her to escape him. In the cramped quarters, we kept colliding with each other.

Zedrick said, as if pleading with me, "See, the police asked me questions, but I screwed up. I should have told them different things. Like, the names of some of the other guys Jonquil had been with, and if they'd been rough with her. But it was right after Jonquil died, and they didn't let me see her, not once, and people were saying that Duncan had killed her, in some kind of drunk rage, or high on drugs, so I believed that, and I didn't want to protect him. There was nobody to take care of me, only the county. Some kind of Children's Aid. Then I was in a foster home, and nobody would talk about it to me. Duncan, he always denied he'd done it. See, where was the knife? They never found the knife. They tried to say he had time to hide it, but they never found any knife. And I knew, I mean I didn't know right away but I figured it out later, that my father would never have killed Jonquil 'cause he wasn't that kind of a man, to hurt a woman. He pushed her around, and slapped her a little, but she pushed back, and slapped harder, Jonquil was a woman who could take care of herself."

Yet she didn't, I thought. Jonquil didn't take care of herself.

Tucking in bedclothes, I felt blood rush into my head. And suddenly I was seeing Momma. In the bathroom of the old house I saw her, stooped over the sink, whimpering to herself. She was trying to wash blood from her face, not bright-red blood but older, dried blood, and there were clots of it in her hair, and a splattering of stains on the daisy print shirt.

Go away! Bad girl! Bad Lorraine.

"Hey!"—Zedrick grabbed at me as I turned to run from the room. I moved blindly, like a frightened animal, hauling the clumsy duffel bag. "Where the fuck are you going? You got no right to walk out while I'm telling you this."

We stumbled together in the hall. I was frantic to get outside, into the fresh night air.

I tried to tell Zedrick that we could discuss it the next day. I was exhausted, I wasn't feeling well, I needed to be alone.

"Well, I don't want to be alone. I got things to say, and you're going to listen."

Zedrick closed his fingers around my wrist, and I managed to shake them off.

Zedrick tugged at my hair, in a gesture I wanted to interpret as playful, big-brother teasing. Before I winced in pain, he released me.

"Lara, hey c'mon. You can sleep in my bed, and I'll sleep out here. I promise."

I stammered, saying that wasn't a good idea. I needed to be alone, I didn't feel well.

"I could make you feel better, honey. Then we could sleep."

Zedrick was crowding against me, giving off a smell of raw hurt, need, sexual arousal. "You were hot enough before. Don't try to say you weren't. Don't be a cocktease, honey. You know you want it, too."

I was gripping both straps of the duffel bag, at chest level. Trying to block Zedrick. We were in the kitchen now, and I was edging toward the opened door. Even in my state of panic I was calculating: could I run, could I run fast enough to get to my car, at the back of the adjacent lot, could I outrun this man, this aroused furious man, and I believed that I could not.

I calculated: should I scream, should I give in to my panic and scream, would I have time to attract anyone's attention before Zedrick clamped a hand over my mouth, or knocked me unconscious, was it worth the risk to scream for help, knowing how Zedrick would react, and I knew that it was not.

"Don't you the fuck *care*? You're his fucking *daughter*."

Zedrick was indignant, too. For I was betraying our father, another time.

Still I was edging toward the door. We were both panting, and staring at each other. With exaggerated caution Zedrick lifted his hands to show how harmless he was, in the way of a teasing elder brother; in this gesture there remained still some small measure of affection. "Hey, Lara: don't you like me? You acted like you did, before."

"Zedrick, of course I—I like you. But I—"

"O.K. then, trust me. I need you with me. I'm not letting you go, I need you really bad."

A glittery madness in his eyes. Our father's eyes. I knew, yet heard myself say, "I can't trust you. You almost killed the Director."

Zedrick smiled, meanly. " 'Director'—who?"

"The Director of the Institute. You must have stalked him, seen him enter the parking garage—"

"Where's this, honey?"

"In Princeton. You know what I'm saying."

"You tell me, honey. Like you know my heart."

"You almost killed him. You're guilty of—"

"Fuck 'guilty.' Who says 'guilty'? There's just you and me."

"An innocent man. A man who never hurt you."

Zedrick laughed. " 'Cause he never had the chance to. 'Cause I found out you were going away together: That's why."

"But—how did you find out? Who told you?"

It must have been Martha. He must have telephoned, made inquiries about me. I saw Zedrick as a man who would always surprise and elude me and whom I could not trust even when he was smiling at me openly and derisively as he was now.

"Look, that fat bastard had no right to you. He had to be stopped. You belong to—someone who knows you."

"But to almost kill him! To—"

"Fucker got in my way, O.K.? Now we're even."

Zedrick laughed, grabbing my wrist. It was a playful struggle, almost; for he seemed to think that, even now, he could win me over, win me back; we'd been teasing each other, as children do; but not to hurt. But then Zedrick was hurting me. His fingers squeezing my arm until I cried out in pain. I kicked at him, tried to wrench away from him, and quick as a flame rushing along a gasoline trail Zedrick put his hands on me, around my rib cage, picked me up with as little effort as if he were picking up a child, and slammed me back against the wall.

In that moment I thought *This is what you deserve, you've provoked this. Now he will murder you.*

Zedrick was saying, "You bitch! Cocktease! Why'd you come here? This is my place, my place I live in, going through my things, laughing at me, think I'm some prick faggot asshole you can push around, what the fuck are you doing here?" He was drunk, his face contorted in hatred. I fumbled for the knife inside the duffel bag, and drew it out, and Zedrick had no idea what I was striking him with, slashing at his hands and forearms, until he saw in astonishment that he was bleeding.

Not to injure him, only just to ward him off.

Not to wound him, only just to protect myself.

Not to kill. Only in self-defense.

Zedrick said, choking, "Jesus! What's this . . . What'd you do . . ."

For a long baffled moment he stood swaying, in the dimly lighted kitchen, staring at his bleeding hands and arms, dark blood dripping onto his work trousers, and onto the linoleum floor. He was utterly confounded as a bear baited by dogs.

"Baby, what'd you do? You cut me? *You cut me?*"

"Get away from me! I'll kill you."

"What? Honey—hey: I wasn't going to hurt you. Why'd you cut me? How'm I gonna work tomorrow?"

I was overcome with shame. Yet I couldn't trust him.

I couldn't leave him bleeding like this, from a dozen surface wounds. I got a kitchen towel and ran water onto it and wrapped it around Zedrick's right hand, that was bleeding more than the other. Still Zedrick stood stunned, now beginning to cry. Zedrick Dewsofski, crying! A choked, painful sound, I realized yes, I'd heard a man cry like this, long ago. It must have been Daddy.

I would drive much of the night, south out of Strykersville. Until I was too exhausted to see, and pulled over at the side of the road, and slept like a weight released into muddy water, and at dawn woke with a jolt to discover that I'd parked beside a deep drainage ditch within sight of the New York State Thruway.

This was the countryside south of Elmira, near the Pennsylvania border.

A halo of pain encased me. Ribs, upper back, neck. The

back of my head. My eyes were seared as if I'd been staring for hours into a fierce light. There were splotches of dried blood on my hands, forearms, clothing and in kinky little snarls in my hair.

The stained steak knife, lying on the car seat beside me, I washed in the ditch and threw as far as I could into the underbrush. Wincing with pain, I couldn't throw it far.

The broken watch still dangling on my wrist, I removed and put away in my bag for safekeeping.

25

18 October 1970: Lake Shaheen, New York

That night. TV voices in the living room. Almost, waking confused you'd think it was Momma talking on the telephone, or Momma talking to herself, laughing her sharp angry laugh like a dog's barking.

Momma warned *That man is hunting us. That man has cast his lot with swine.*

When I wakened I did not know was it day, was it night. I did not know where my brother Ryan was, who'd been standing barefoot in the opened doorway looking toward the road waiting for headlights in the dark. The TV voices were gone.

I stumbled from my bed scared and needing to pee. There was Momma in the bathroom bent over the sink. Sobbing, talking to herself. Trying to lift water in her hands, to wash her face. I was so scared: seeing blood on Momma's pretty face, not bright-red blood but dried blood. And there was blood in Momma's hair like patches of paint.

Bloodstains on Momma's daisy-print shirt like my own.

I believed that Momma had been hurt and Momma was going to die and I began crying and Momma's eyes snatched at mine through the mirror.

Go away! Bad girl! Bad Lorraine.

Go away, don't look, this isn't for you to see, bad girl!

And the back of Momma's hand swiping my face so quick my face was struck blank as a doll's.

26

---

11 June 1993:
Las Vegas, Nevada

Not an ideal time of the year to visit Nevada, Ryan warned over the phone.

Yet I flew to Las Vegas in early summer. Into the blast-furnace sun. I could not explain to Ryan that there would be no ideal time for me, for what I had to know.

I had not seen Ryan for so many years, I worried I wouldn't recognize him. But when at the Las Vegas airport a tall lanky youngish man with a prematurely lined face stepped forward to greet me, I knew him at once.

We were self-conscious, clumsy. We shook hands at first, then hugged. Then we laughed, in nervous relief.

"I was afraid I wouldn't know you."

"I was afraid I w-wouldn't know *you*."

Not the drug-wasted old-young man with sunken eyes I had envisioned in my nightmare speculation of our meeting but a seemingly healthy man of medium build, looking not much older than his age of thirty-one, stood before me, smiling. An edgy smile but a welcoming smile, I believed. (The missing teeth had been replaced by a row of shiny white teeth neat as plastic.) Ryan Quade, whom I'd last seen in prison-issue pajamas in the Men's House of Detention in Phoenix, was now wearing a white shirt with short sleeves, clean khaki shorts, sandals; on his head, which looked prim and small since he seemed to have very little hair, a white baseball cap with prominent green stitching: DECATUR HOUSE. (Decatur House was the halfway house where, as I'd discovered through numerous telephone calls, Ryan lived and had a position as assistant director of a Nevada state-funded drug rehabilitation program. My junkie brother!) His handshake had been firm. He held himself in the erect, stiff posture of one whose motor coordination isn't wholly predictable, but you could see that this was a man who had a measure of confidence in himself, if not vanity.

Later, Ryan would acknowledge, yes he was looking good for where he'd been, what he'd come through. In some quarters Ryan Quade was a kind of poster child for the miracle of rehabilitation: "If it worked for him, it can work for anybody. Though it didn't hurt, Jesus loved him." Ryan's laughter sounded like fingernails scraping a blackboard, but at a distance: you knew what the sound was, and your skin prickled, but you also knew that it wasn't nearly so bad as it could be.

Walking without hesitation, no limp or drag to his left foot, Ryan led me briskly through the small, very chill airport where tourist-gamblers were already at slot machines. Avid, eager. You could envy them their child-like absorption. I hated gambling: the idiot hope of "winning" that mimicked other kinds of hope, so painfully raw, exposed. At the same time I recognized my hatred as a kind of fear, and I didn't understand this fear. *Risk? Any risk, you'll be hurt.*

At one of the slot machines I saw a glamorous woman in her sixties with a spun-gold 1970s bouffant head, for a quick anxious moment reminding me of Hedy, though Hedy had never been blond, had never worn her hair in such an exaggerated style nor had she ever worn snakeskin pedal pushers and matching shoes, so far as I knew. As Ryan and I passed behind her, the woman squealed in delight to her Stetson-hat white-goatee companion as the slot machine burst into tinkly jackpot music and a modest stream of coins fell into her opened hands. *Like semen* the thought came to me unbidden, and was at once repulsed.

I saw that, here in Nevada where I had never been before, I was in a new world, where chance ruled. Or there was the collective wish that chance, and not rigged machines, ruled.

"Why did you come here, Ryan? Why Vegas?"

My voice was light, enthusiastic. I was my brother's guest in this place for four days, and would not judge.

"Why—here?" Ryan glanced around, with a distracted smile. We were in the parking lot, in blinding sunshine, at a white minivan that belonged to Decatur House; alarming to me, yet fascinating, how the dry, whitish sunshine shimmered and shook in waves of heat. "You mean, Decatur House itself, or—Las Vegas, Nevada?"

"Both."

"Because this is where I ended up, Lorraine. I mean, Lara. This is where I was washed ashore. You could say that I was born here. Reborn."

Reborn. I wasn't sure what this meant, and didn't want to ask.

As I hadn't wanted to ask about Hedy, so soon. But on the way into Las Vegas, Ryan told me, yes Hedy was alive, not in perfect health but alive; in fact, he'd brought her from Phoenix two years ago to live in an assisted-care facility a few miles from Decatur House.

"Momma is here? Living *here*?"

This was stunning news. I had not expected this, since on the phone, when I'd failed to ask after Hedy, Ryan had volunteered no information.

"Lara, don't laugh. Momma's in a suburb called 'Paradise.' "

I didn't laugh. I was staring at the side of my brother's face as he drove, somewhat stiffly, ramrod straight behind the steering wheel, through walls of dazzling sunshine. In the near distance, lifting like mirages out of the desert, were high-rise hotels and casinos looking flat as paper cutouts against the haze-smudged sky.

Ryan said, without irony, "The Strip looks its best at night. Not now."

Ryan's life was now Decatur House. He helped supervise forty-nine residents, all of them former drug addicts and many of them ex-alcoholics. And ex-convicts. Most would have been homeless except for the halfway house. Many were mentally disturbed, borderline schizophrenics and bipolar sufferers dependent upon continuous medication. Ryan said quietly, "This is my mission. I'm meant to be here. Jesus brought me to this. Every minute, I give thanks for my life."

At first Ryan's allusions to Jesus, as to rebirth, had seemed playful and conversational, but I'd come to see that my brother was a serious believer. He spoke of Jesus having entered his heart at a time when he'd been given up for dead, and all of his life— "forward and back"—had been transformed at that moment. He'd been twenty-six at the time. On March 2, it had been five years. He met with a small group of like-minded Christians in the area, some of whom worked at Decatur House, some in the casinos, who had dedicated themselves to be "subversive" Christians: "We strive to live like Christ, but not speak of it."

I stared at Ryan in dismay. How derisive my brother had been as an adolescent, of our mother's TV evangelicals, her soppy Jesus and frantic prayers. Almost, I felt that he'd betrayed me. He had always been so much more wounded than I, so much more sardonic, lacking in hope. Closer to the edge.

"Like I'm a junkie whether I ever shoot up again, I'm a Christian even if I cease to believe. Jesus allowed me to know this, Lara. It doesn't depend upon believing every minute of every day because Jesus isn't going to vanish if I don't believe, see? Like Death Valley is there if you know it or not." Ryan was speaking quietly, but with passion. "This knowledge has brought me such peace, you can't imagine."

"Yes. I can imagine."

But dimly, as you imagine a foreign setting you've never seen.

Ryan said, "At Decatur House, if a patient asks for the New Testament, I provide it. But I don't say much, not like I'm talking now, for what's to say? Grace comes into the heart like lightning. If it's going to come at all."

Ryan spoke so matter-of-factly, as if he were telling me the time, I wanted to laugh.

And yet I felt sad, hearing his words, for I knew that my brother was right, and I knew that grace would never come into my heart. Not like lightning nor even in slow grudging drips like one of our giant icicles thawing in Lake Shaheen, in late winter.

I told Ryan that I'd never been capable of believing in another world, I had all I could do to believe in this world. At the Institute in Princeton where I was, or had been, a research fellow, the very world (always set off in quotation marks to designate it as a mental construct, "world") was explored as a semiotic phenomenon; the sum of myriad human projections and wishes. And so, it was impossible for me to believe in yet another construct.

Ryan said, as if this wasn't pretentious babble but quite reasonable, "Lara, I know. After our mother's example, who in hell would want to be 'religious'? Her Jesus was just self-pity. At the time we were too young to know. Religion was just one more delusion of Hedy's, like her alcohol addiction, her shame, and her guilt. It had nothing to do with any other human being, not even her children, and it certainly had nothing to do with Christ."

Ryan spoke with something of his old adolescent scorn. I could see his left eyelid twitching.

Emotion shimmered between us like the hot Nevada air. I chose my words carefully, uncertain how Ryan might respond.

"That night, Ryan, when the woman in Good Hope was killed, do you remember? We didn't know at the time, of course. We were just children. But that night—when Momma—" My voice began to falter. I wasn't sure what I meant to say. I was hearing Zedrick Dewsofski's furious voice *I want the fucker who killed her to be punished, I'd like to sink a knife in a few times, myself.* "Daddy was arrested and convicted and everybody seemed to think he must be guilty. But he never confessed, did he? He'd always said he was innocent. Do you know—do you think—it's possible—"

"That Hedy killed her? Yes."

Now the words were uttered, my brother and I regarded each other almost calmly. The tension in my heart relaxed. *It has been said. It can't be unsaid.*

" 'Lara.' I like your new name. It's like music."

We were driving along Las Vegas Boulevard in the early evening.

After the ferocity of the sun had faded, at the mountainous horizon a pulsing disc like neon. You could watch the sun "set" in the west by perceptible degrees but of course there was no ensuing darkness, not in Vegas. Here, the night came alive like fireworks.

It was the third day of my visit. I would be leaving in less than twenty-four hours. I had not yet seen Hedy. I had asked few questions about her, in the Paradise Valley Manor. Ryan had told me that she was "changed"—"you might say, transformed"—much older than she'd been when I saw her last, of course, and weakened by years of drinking, smoking, abusing her body. "She's had cirrhosis, and she's had—well, she has, cancer. It started in her lungs, and metastasized. Chemotherapy almost killed her, wasn't helping her, so she's off, now. Most days she knows who I am. I see her two-three times a week. Not out of duty, Lara. But because I want to bring her peace."

Peace! My mouth twisted in hurt, derision.

"But you think she killed that woman. 'Jonquil.' "

"Yes. I can't know it, and I can't ask her. I don't think that Momma drove to Good Hope that night with the intention of killing, but—I think it must have happened that way. She'd left the house that night. Later, I would figure out the date: October 18, 1970. The night that 'Jonquil' was stabbed to death. It wasn't that far a drive, really—if you drove fast, each way wouldn't have been more than forty minutes; but it seemed a longer distance somehow, because of needing to drive south around the lake. You must have heard her on the phone, Lorraine—"

Had I? I wasn't sure what Ryan meant.

"Momma would be on the phone saying, 'You have no right to him. He's my husband, he's the father of my children. Leave him alone!' She'd hang up, and dial again, and finally the other party wasn't answering, and she'd get drunk, her radio music up high, and the TV on—she made us go to bed early. That night, I went to bed but I didn't sleep. I was watching TV and waiting for her. I was outside, on the road. I can remember it was October, because Hallowe'en was coming up. We used to look forward to Hallowe'en, remember? It wasn't just that one time Momma went away at night, but that was one of the times, afterward she'd de-nied she went out, then she admitted, yes she'd gone out but just to talk with Daddy in the car, and maybe they'd driven around some, we were asleep, and we woke up, and we tried to stay awake, and next thing I knew she was home, it must have been after 3 A.M., Momma was in the bathroom trying to wash blood off her face, her hands. We were terrified, we thought the blood was hers. She'd kept saying how our father was hunting her, wanting to hurt her. But it wasn't Hedy's blood, it was her victim's blood." Ryan paused, now breathing hard. Having to add, quietly, "This is what I think, Lorraine. Not what I know."

" 'Lara.' "

"Sorry! 'Lara.' "

Ryan braked suddenly as a convertible sports car like a shiny red beetle cut in front of us, passing on the right. I was thrown forward against my shoulder belt, and pain shot through my ribs and upper body like flame.

"Lara? Are you all right?"

"Yes. Yes. I'm fine."

My eyes filled with moisture, I had to keep wiping away. Not tears exactly. Not tears of sorrow, or hurt. I was remembering the back of a hand slapping my face so swiftly, I'd hardly known that I'd been struck. *Bad girl! Go away. Spying on me.*

"Do you think he knew? Our father?"

"Maybe."

"Yet he didn't accuse her. He took the blame for her."

"How can we know? We can't know."

"Did he give the police the names of anybody else, who might have killed Jonquil? I don't think he did. I think he just denied he'd done it, that was his defense."

" 'Duncan Quade.' Our father, who's been dead so long. Don't you think, sometimes, Lara, it was only just something that could have happened back there, and at that time?"

" 'Back there'—?"

"In Lake Shaheen. In Good Hope. In that time." Ryan laughed, hunching his shoulders behind the wheel. "That's why I would never return east. I'd lose my faith, maybe. I'd lose myself. There's too much family history. In Nevada, especially in Vegas, time plays out differently. Like in the casinos there are no clocks, and no windows; it's always brightly lighted, and noisy. At Decatur House, we emphasize the present tense and the future. What's past is past. What's past is definitely past. You can learn from your past but then you move on, and you try not to look back."

I said, stubbornly, "She destroyed our lives, not just an innocent woman's life. She destroyed our father's life."

"And her own life, too, Lara."

But she's still alive. She sucked life from us.

"Ryan, we could talk to her. Confront her."

"Yes, Lara. We could."

"Take me—take me with you? To see her? Tomorrow morning?"

My flight was leaving in the late afternoon. A red-eye, overnight, to Newark.

Ryan nodded yes. He'd take me. Of course.

"Is Momma—Hedy—very ill? She'll know me, won't she?"

Ryan drove, not taking his eyes off the boulevard.

We were passing such phantasmagoric sights! A frenzy of neon and swirling lights. Through waves of amplified pop music. Like cathedrals and mosques of exotic religions the high-rise hotels and gambling casinos floated past: the Sahara, and the Barbary Coast, and the Golden Nugget, and the Oasis, and the

Rainbow, and Caesar's Palace, and the Pyramid, and Vegas World immense and glittering as a manic grin. Ryan said, "Vegas World used to be Hedy's favorite. I'd take her out sometimes, when she could still walk. We never gambled of course. Not even the slots. We'd ride on the moving sidewalks and escalators and sit and watch the tourists. Vegas World is basically a circus in a casino, always lots of children. Hedy loved the children."

I was stunned to hear this. *Hedy loved the children, whose children?*

I saw that my brother was smiling. I resented that smile.

My ex-junkie born-again Christian brother, I resented.

27

12 June 1993:
Paradise, Nevada

Next morning Ryan drove me to Paradise Valley Manor to visit our mother.

I'd been awake much of the night. I had lain in my bed in the dark observing the undersea play of lights and shadows on the ceiling of the room thinking *I can't do this, I must do this.* For otherwise why had I come to this place. Why had I re-entered my brother's precariously maintained life, except to wrest a vestige of truth out of the lies of our past.

I would never see Zedrick Dewsofski again, I thought. Yet I owed it to him, to determine who had killed his mother.

Ryan hadn't wanted me to stay in a motel, he'd insisted upon putting me up at Decatur House, where he lived. A guest room adjacent to his small quarters. As assistant director, Ryan Quade was the resident at the house with the most authority, since the director lived elsewhere. Twenty-four hours a day, Ryan was on call.

"It's my life. I'm grateful for my life."

Through the night I thought of Ryan, and my resentment of

him: for he'd known, or guessed, that Hedy had killed the woman in Good Hope, and not our father; and he had not told me. *Wanting to spare you. Don't hate him.* My brother had been in contact with Hedy over the years when I had assumed (out of chagrin, guilt) that he too had ceased to see her. Yet he'd never confronted her.

"I will confront her. It's time."

Nearly twenty-three years since a woman named Jonquil Dewsofski had been stabbed to death. Two dozen stab wounds. Imagine the fury, the hatred. Imagine the blood.

Beside my bed, an antiquated window air conditioner rattled, dripped water, emitted a barely cooled stale-smelling air into my face.

"How was your night?" Ryan asked in the morning, and I said, as I invariably did, smiling, "Fine! It was fine."

On the way to Paradise Valley Manor, impulsively I told Ryan about our half-brother: "His name is 'Zedrick.' Daddy's other son."

Why I'd chosen this moment to tell Ryan, I don't know. I had not known what I would say until I began speaking.

We were driving in white-hot sunshine that shattered and glared off a thousand shiny surfaces. The white minivan, though not shiny-clean, glared as if radioactive.

For a moment Ryan was too surprised to react. Then, unusual for him, he took his eyes off the road, glancing at me in disbelief.

" 'H-Half-brother'? 'Zedrick'? My God."

"I—I thought you might have known, Ryan. Known something."

"Do you have pictures of him?"

It was such a natural response, yet unexpected. Keenly I felt the loss, that I had no pictures of Zedrick Dewsofski to show Ryan.

I told Ryan no, I was sorry that I did not. But maybe I could get some.

"His name is—'Zedrick'? Is his last name—'Quade'?"

"No. His mother's name was 'Dewsofski.' "

The name seemed to pass Ryan by, he was too distracted to hear.

I began to regret telling him this news at such an inopportune time.

Ryan said, trying not to become overexcited, "How did you meet him, Lara? Did he find you?"

"Yes, he came to see me. In Princeton."

"Princeton! When was this?"

"In April. He wants to meet you, too. He wants to meet his brother Ryan, he says, very badly."

"I want to meet him, too. My God."

Though adding, "But I—I'm not going back east. He'd have to come here."

"Well, maybe he will. He seemed very serious about meeting you."

My account of Zedrick Dewsofski was veering into improbability, fantasy. I could not seem to control it. I was an eager child who'd handed a friend a balloon, the friend had snatched at the balloon and now it was rising out of the reach of both.

Ryan was saying, uneasily, "This 'Zedrick'—is he the son of the woman who was k-killed? The woman called 'J-Jonquil'?"

So he does know, I thought. He must have heard rumors.

"Yes, he is."

"My God."

Ryan shook his head, stymied. The white baseball cap with the green letters DECATUR HOUSE, pulled low over his forehead to help shield his eyes from the sun, gave him an inappropriate jaunty air; his thin face was leathery, lined, and now unsmiling. I had wanted to draw our attention away from our mother in the nursing home, but I had succeeded too well.

Ryan asked how old Zedrick was. I said I wasn't sure— "Maybe a little older than you."

"Older!" Ryan stared as if he were driving into a blizzard, blind. I could see my brother trying frantically to calculate what this might mean but failing, baffled. "But how could he be— older? He's got to be a lot younger."

I said nothing. Ryan had been taking for granted that Duncan Quade's other family, in Good Hope, if he'd had one, had existed in the aftermath of his separation from Hedy. He would have supposed Zedrick Dewofski to be no older than twenty-two, born after 1970.

I said, "At least, he looks older. He has a sort of battered face."

"Battered? Has he been—injured?"

Like us Ryan meant. Quickly I told him no.

I wondered how far we had to drive yet, to Paradise. Traffic was slowed on the southbound expressway where an exit leading to the suburb of Winchester was blocked. Ryan had become agitated, distracted. I had seen at Decatur House how composed he was there: that 1950s stucco domicile of posted rules and regulations, scheduled mealtimes, therapies, and curfews, routines as comforting as those of an elementary school. Outside Decatur House, Ryan was less certain. I had to make amends.

"Zedrick, sometimes called 'Zed.' He seems to have been brought up in a commune. On an old farm in Good Hope. He works with his hands and he takes pride in his work but he's an artist, too. You would admire his paintings—"

As I spoke of our brother to Ryan, for the remainder of the drive to Paradise Valley Manor, the man became increasingly unreal to me; far less real than the man who dwelled in my memory with a vividness and an intensity like pain. Hearing my description of him, Zedrick would have sneered. The Director, a theorist who doubted all "eyewitness" accounts of so-called "reality," was certainly right: to be a witness to anyone or anything is to distort, however well-intentioned one is.

But I could not tell Ryan the truth about our half-brother: that he was unstable, dangerous. A potential killer. (Had he killed, already? I wouldn't have been surprised.) I could not tell Ryan that Zedrick had been wounded by the cataclysm of our family more severely than Ryan and I had been. Instead, I found myself telling Ryan an entertaining tale of how Zedrick had driven to Princeton from Strykersville, New York, where he lived, to meet me, since he'd heard from mutual relatives that I was living now in Princeton. In this version, there was no trickery in-volving a ticket sent to L Quade, and there was certainly no men-tion of the drunken assault in my apartment. I did not tell Ryan about the brutal beating of the Director, and I did not tell him of my driving to Strykersville to retrieve our father's broken watch. Or of Zedrick convincing me that Duncan Quade had not been the one to murder his mother.

To confess such things to Ryan would be to implicate myself in Zedrick's madness. And I had come to Las Vegas with the hope of ridding myself of all madness.

"He's a painter? You said? What kind of paintings?"

"Strange, eerie. Beautiful, I think. They're of clouds."

"Clouds!"

Ryan laughed, enjoying this. More and more he was coming to like his newly discovered brother with the bizarre archaic name.

"Mostly the kinds of clouds you see in the sky back home. Those heavy thunderheads over Lake Ontario, remember?" Above the smoggy expressway the Nevada sky was a featureless bleached-out blue but Ryan and I shuddered seeing again the great storm clouds moving like predators above the lake, inland; those shark-shapes that floated like bad dreams beneath our wak-ing lives. "The paintings remind me of certain works of Magritte, but Zedrick has probably never seen Magritte. I suppose he'd be categorized as a 'primitive.' His art is 'outsider art.' Some of the most ambitious paintings, he's never finished. He has to support himself as a carpenter and a house painter, it must be frustrating to live in such isolation in a place remote as Strykersville."

"Zedrick had lived in Good Hope until—?"

"Yes."

"Did he say much to you about the—murder?"

"We didn't talk about the murder."

"He must have asked you lots of questions about us. About Daddy."

"No. I think Zedrick wants to forget, as we do."

I was hoping that Ryan would let this go, for the time being.

Still he persisted: "How old was he when—it happened?"

"I really don't know."

"He wasn't just a baby, I guess? He was old enough to—know?"

"He wasn't there that night, with his mother. He was somewhere else."

"Where did he live, after—? With relatives?"

"Yes, I'm sure. With relatives."

Telling such lies I was beginning to sweat. I resented having to tell such lies! I told my brother that Zedrick wanted to forget the past. I told him that Zedrick was an idealist, an artist. "He says he'll always be an artist even if he stops painting, because he believes in beauty, and beauty is always there in the world, whether we acknowledge it or not."

"He said that? Zedrick?"

Ryan almost missed the Paradise Road exit, he was so caught up in our conversation.

At the Paradise Valley Manor things became undersea.

As soon as we entered the Spanish-style stucco building that looked as if it had been built shortly after World War II.

As soon as we breathed in the lukewarm air that smelled of disinfectant, air freshener, dried urine, and something very sweet like vanilla.

As soon as Ryan murmured in my ear, "Lara, be prepared. Our mother isn't the same person you might remember."

I wanted to say, annoyed *I know that! I'm not a child.*

Here I was bringing Hedy a potted hydrangea. Clusters of unnatural-looking blue flowers. This offering in a tinfoil-wrapped clay pot I held awkwardly in my arms, embraced against my chest.

I couldn't hear very clearly. Sounds, voices were muffled in my ears. My heartbeat was erratic as a moth's flailing wings. The air was thick and viscous as murky water.

"Lara. We'll have to call you Lorraine."

Ryan took my hand, gently pulling me forward.

I would notice that in the Manor, my brother had begun to walk less certainly than he walked elsewhere. A slight limp, a drag to his left foot.

At the visitors' desk we were issued passes. At a heavy plate-glass door, Ryan punched in a code. E-Ward. What was E-Ward?

We followed a corridor, and another corridor. The smells intensified. Through an opened doorway I saw, or thought I saw, a mannequin seated in a chair, immobile. One of those white-bandaged faceless figures you see in contemporary art museums, by the sculptor George Segal.

Ryan led me into a day lounge where elderly patients, some in wheelchairs, were watching TV, or staring toward a TV set, or staring into space, or, at a long table, overseen by a stocky dark-skinned nurse's aide, appeared to be sewing, knitting. The materials in which they worked were bright primary colors.

When my vision adjusted to this undersea room I saw that not all of these patients were elderly; one or two were not much older than Ryan and me. Yet most had eggshell heads overlarge for their wasted bodies.

I saw to my relief that Hedy wasn't here.

"Lara? Here."

Gently, Ryan pulled me toward the table. He took the hydrangea from my arms and set it down in front of one of the eggshell-head women. In a cheerful-Christian voice he said, "Momma? Hello! This is your son Ryan, and this is your daughter Lorraine come to visit. Lorraine has brought you this plant, Momma."

A woman shrunken to the size of a prepubescent child, weighing perhaps seventy-five pounds, peered up at me startled. Her eyes were magnified through thick-lensed glasses that looked too heavy for her fragile face. Ryan said, louder, "Momma? I'm your son Ryan, and this is your daughter Lorraine come to visit you. You remember Lorraine, Momma, we haven't seen Lorraine in a while but—h-here she is."

I was stunned. The undersea sensation intensified, I was having trouble breathing.

Yet I heard myself say, "*Momma! Hello.*"

I saw my hands reach out to my mother's hands, that had been holding something fashioned out of pink yarn fabric; not to hold her hands but just to touch, stroke. These were sparrow-boned hands, disfigured by prominent blue veins across the knuckles.

I was recalling what Ryan had told me, about which I had not further inquired. *Cirrhosis, cancer. Lungs, metastasized. Chemotherapy.* "Momma? It's Lorraine. I—I've missed you."

The woman's lips twitched in a kind of smile. Her mouth appeared to be toothless, collapsed. Her head was covered in a fine dull-gray fuzz like lichen. Her face wasn't so much lined and creased as collapsed, like raw bread dough.

I calculated: Hedy Quade was in her early fifties.

This woman wasn't Hedy, and wasn't Momma. Yet as Ryan had said, she was our mother. Someone pulled out a chair for me, I sat close beside her. In the murky undersea air we had to squint at each other, to see.

I told my mother again that I'd missed her. I'd been thinking of her. I was living and working now in New Jersey but I'd just been back—*back home* I was going to say but reconsidered. And maybe it would be a mistake, to speak of her sister Agnes?

My mother wasn't hearing much of these faltering words. Yet I think she recognized me now. She smiled, and touched my cheek. She tried to speak but only a papery rustling sound issued from her throat.

Ryan leaned between us to murmur in my ear, "Momma has had an esophagectomy, Lara."

A word I'd never heard before. Yet I didn't have to ask my brother what it meant.

The visit with my mother lasted less than fifteen minutes. We managed to communicate, in a way. My face was damp with tears but I was smiling: I think I must have been happy. In such circumstances you float like a cork on the buoyancy of whatever element you find yourself in. You say whatever words come to you. "Momma, it's so good to see you! Momma, I love you." Before we left, my mother gave me the pink object she'd been making, and I thanked her, and walked slowly away, and when I looked back at the entrance to the lounge I saw that my mother's eyes were closed, she was slumped in her chair like a rag doll.

I seemed to know: I would never again be haunted by the embittered, deranged woman accelerating her car downhill to the railway crossing at Lake Shaheen. I would never again dream of the drunken woman lying naked on her bed, or in scummy bathwater, or on the worn-out carpet in front of the air conditioner in our rental in Phoenix, a glisten of saliva on her mouth. I thought *Hedy is gone. No one will ever know her guilt.*

In the parking lot Ryan told me that the cirrhosis had burnt out much of Hedy's memory, even before the cancer. "Already she'd forgetting us. It's like footprints in the sand, filling in with water. What did she give you?"

I held it out for Ryan to see: a pink sock doll with button eyes and strips of flannel for a nose and mouth. The stitches in the flannel, made with pink thread darker than the pink yarn material of the doll, were prominent as surgical stitches.

"I used to think she'd buried the knife, the bloody clothes. Out in her garden, remember Momma's garden? I don't know if I saw her with a shovel the next morning, or dreamt it. I don't know if I was awake when she came home stumbling and crying that night, or dreamt it. But I always did think there was another boy—a boy like me—but more special than me—living on the other side of the lake, and that was why Daddy left us, he loved that boy more than he loved me. When you're a child there are things you believe to be true that are fantasies, but there are things you think are fantasies that turn out to be true." Ryan paused, and before I could reply he began talking about our mother's garden. Did I remember? Out behind the house? The old wire fence, where grape vines grew? Momma's hollyhocks, sweet peas, tomato plants, pole beans. "Overnight in July there'd be so many pole beans! Momma sent us out to pick them, 'Be sure to look under the leaves,' Momma would say. It was always a surprise how fast they grew. You'd think you had picked every damn bean, but there were always a few you'd missed. Remember, Lorraine?"

Ryan was driving me to the Las Vegas airport. He'd begun to speak rapidly, excitedly. I wanted to touch him, to comfort him. I was afraid to look at his face, that I might see a tremor beginning. I was fearful of Ryan drifting into oncoming traffic, overcome by a sudden seizure. Though I wasn't sure what I remembered of our mother's garden I said, "Yes, Ryan! I remember."

■■■

28

23 June 1993:
Lake Shaheen/Strykersville,
New York

I returned to Lake Shaheen. I returned to the old house on route 39. I intended to dig in the garden.

Since Ryan had said he'd seen Momma with a shovel, it had come to seem to me, yes I'd seen her, too.

When I knocked at the screen door, a teenaged girl came to open it. Gaping at me when I introduced myself, made my request.

I used to live here, I told her. A long time ago.

May I walk around outside? May I see the garden?

Sure, the girl said. Nobody's home but me, me and my baby brother, sure go ahead. My name's Lacey.

Lacey had been on the phone giggling when I'd knocked. The receiver, she held in the crook of her chin and shoulder. Lacey wore a tiny black halter top, tight vinyl shorts in a zebra stripe, she was barefoot and each of her finger- and toenails was painted a different color. Her hair was a mane of fawn-brown and purple streaks.

Out back of the house, there was no garden. Just grass.

Children's swings, an above-ground swimming pool with a badly stained plastic covering. Beyond the carport, a toolshed. Someone cared enough about the crabgrass lawn to now it, and someone cared enough about flowers to set out petunias and pansies around the house, but there was no garden of the kind Momma had had. I tried to remember where the garden might have been, and wasn't sure. I smiled at the futility of my quest.

If I wanted to dig here, if I received permission from the home-owner to undertake such a task, I would dig in that hard grassy ground with a shovel until my hands bled, even with gloves. I would dig, dig, dig until my shoulders and back were wracked with pain. I would dig in the hot sunshine until my head pounded with migraine. And I would find nothing: probably.

Rotted clothes, after more than twenty years? An old rusted knife?

A rotted rubber doll with a bald head?

She's just standing there the girl's voice wafted to me from inside the house. *No I told you, I never seen her before.*

After a few minutes I returned to the house. Strange for me to think of this as our old house when in fact it was someone else's new house. Smart beige siding, sunny-yellow shutters. Carport with rose trellises.

I called politely to Lacey through the screen door, Thanks!

She came to the door to stare after me, perplexed but smiling. The last I saw of the girl she lifted a hand in farewell as I backed my car out of the driveway.

So close to Strykersville, less than one hundred miles: might as well drive there.

The thought came to me *I will leave a bottle of Gordon's gin on his back step.*

I owed him, after all.

There was nowhere else I wanted to be. Back in Princeton my apartment remained empty. It was said of the Director that he was "convalescing" at home. I had not seen him since the assault but I had tried to telephone him, once. Whoever answered the phone, a nurse or an assistant, told me solemnly that it would be some time yet before the Director could speak on the phone.

I asked to be remembered to him. Though knowing the Director would remember nothing of me, not even my name.

Since visiting my brother Ryan, admiring his new life at Decatur House, I'd begun to think that I might quit the academic world. I might return to upstate New York. I could teach in a public school: I'd found it challenging to assist a volunteer remedial reading instructor at Decatur House, one-on-one tutoring that was painstaking and exhausting but more satisfying than typing on a computer or researching esoteric material at the Institute for a "brilliant critic" to pass off as his own.

At the Vegas airport, my parting with Ryan had been emotional.

Half-jokingly he'd asked me to come back, soon. To come join the staff of Decatur House with him.

But I preferred upstate New York.

At 6 P.M. I stopped for gas and telephoned Zedrick Dewsofski and the phone rang unanswered.

At 7 P.M. on the outskirts of Strykersville I stopped at a liquor store to buy the bottle of gin, and dialed Zedrick's number another time. No answer.

I wasn't impatient. I wasn't anxious. I thought *He's here. He hasn't left.*

I drove along Canal Road. When I passed the gaunt old gunmetal-gray farmhouse it appeared that no one was home: no rust-edged Cutlass in the driveway, no downstairs lights. I seemed to have decided not to leave the bottle of gin on Zedrick's back step.

At 9 P.M. from a pay phone outside a 7-Eleven store I dialed not Zedrick's number but the number of the Canal House and asked for Zedrick Dewsofski and amid a blast of noise Zedrick was summoned to the phone.

His voice was suspicious—"Yeah? Who's this?"

I told him. His sister Lara.

There was a moment's silence. I shut my eyes: saw Zedrick stroking his hair roughly, staring and blinking.

He recovered from his surprise. Guardedly he said, with an air of teasing reproach, "About time you called, Lara. I've been missing you."

He asked where I was, and I told him. He asked was I going to drop by his place, and I said I thought I might, yes. If I was invited.

Sure I was invited, he said. How soon could I get there?

In about three minutes, I told him. But I couldn't stay the night.